SO MANY QUESTIONS, SUCH FRIGHTENING ANSWERS

Andrea's aristocratic husband was so kindly and gentle—but why did unpredictable rages flood through him like madness itself?

The beautiful blue room that Andrea slept in alone was so enchanting—but why had the windows once been barred?

The cynical wit and arrogance of Andrea's darkly handsome stepson should have filled her with distaste—but why did she find herself trembling like a schoolgirl at his glance?

The father who had abandoned Andrea so long ago clearly had no use for her—but why did he send her so urgent a message of warning?

Andrea had a title and a position far beyond her youthful years—and was caught in a maze of mystery and mischief that demanded she grow up swiftly if she were to survive. . . .

THE AUTUMN COUNTESS

The Autumn Countess

Catherine Coulter

A SIGNET BOOK

NEW AMERICAN LIBRARY

A DIVISION OF PENGUIN BOOKS USA INC.

Copyright © 1978 by Catherine Coulter

SIGNET, SIGNET CLASSIC, MENTOR, ONYX, PLUME, MERIDIAN
and NAL BOOKS are published by New American Library, a division of
Penguin Books USA Inc., 1633 Broadway, New York, New York 10019

First Signet Printing, January, 1979

7   8   9   10   11   12   13   14

PRINTED IN THE UNITED STATES OF AMERICA

TO
CSABA

ONE

I was slouched in a tangled, unladylike position in Grandfather's big leather chair, reading about my hero, Lord Nelson. I had spent many happy hours with Grandfather discussing his naval feats. "A man's man he was," Grandfather had declared, "and a true English gentlemen, not one of those namby-pamby foreigners." And, sometimes, when Grandfather was feeling a bit wicked, he would regale me with spicy stories of the notorious Lady Hamilton. "A rare piece she was, that's for sure! Led the admiral a merry chase."

"Drea, where the devil are you?" I looked up at my brother in astonishment. There was obvious anger in his voice, and Mrs. Pringe, Grandfather's housekeeper, eyed him with interest as she let herself reluctantly out of the library.

"Really, Peter," I said with asperity, "you know Mrs. Pringe is the greatest gossip below stairs in London!

1

Please contain yourself until she is at least beyond the keyhole!"

Peter cast an impatient glance over his shoulder at the library door as he strode over to me, a deep scowl on his handsome face. "Damn, Drea, I have just this hour heard of this great folly you have committed! I want to know what the devil has gotten into you!"

"My dear brother, I have no idea what this 'great folly' can be. Tell me," I added cordially, "what glaring solecism have I committed now?"

I knew very well what Peter was talking about, but was not about to say so. I had to proceed carefully, for he had a quick temper.

"Really, Peter," I cried playfully, "how could you sully my virgin ears with such language! 'Tis hardly fit for a lady's drawing room."

Peter seemed to struggle with himself for a moment and finally grinned at me. He was still upset and angry, but now he was controlled.

"I repeat, Andrea," he said in a calmer voice, "what the devil has gotten into you? And don't try to sidetrack the issue, as you do so well, for you know full well what I'm talking about!"

"Very well," I affirmed, "of course I know what you're referring to, and now that you are over your tantrum, we can discuss this reasonably . . . like two grown people." My voice was a hopeful question. I prayed that I did not sound stilted and rehearsed, for I had been practicing. I wanted so desperately not to make a mull of it. Peter was all the family I had left, and I loved him dearly.

"Before we convene a family council, would you like a glass of port?" As I spoke, I untangled myself, rose from the chair, and walked to the sideboard.

"Devilish cool about this, aren't you, little sister?" Peter was himself again, and I saw him frown amiably as I poured a glass of port for myself, as well. "Drea, how many times do I have to tell you that a lady don't drink port? Dammit, that's only for men! Can't you make do with some Madeira . . . or ratafia?" he asked hopefully.

"No, my dear, it tastes like pap, as you well know," I said with a scowl. "I fail to see what my being female has to do with taste in drink." I handed him his glass, and grinning, raised mine in a toast.

"You're a baggage, Andrea." He sighed as he clicked his glass against mine.

"Now," I said encouragingly, feeling fortified by the port, "come and sit with me." I walked over to a sofa, sat down, and patted the place beside me.

Peter stretched his graceful form beside me, reached his hand to my arm, and gave it a shake. "You're incorrigible, Drea." He looked thoughtful for a moment, set down his glass, and took my hand in his. "I've come from Grandfather's advocate, Craigsdale, you see, and I know," he said heavily. As if to allow me time to collect myself, he added, "By the way, I suppose you know already that you're a very rich young lady?"

"Yes," I answered quietly. My hand tensed in his, waiting.

"Toward the end of our meeting, Craigsdale apologized to me for being so forgetful and offered me his congratulations. You know Craigsdale has gotten a bit rusty in his upper works lately, and I assumed he was confused again. I just looked at him blankly, and he said in his flurried way, 'Oh, dear, I assumed, that is, I thought for certain that your charming sister would have told you!'

" 'Told me what, my dear sir?' I asked. 'Why,' he sputtered, 'that she's accepted the Earl of Devbridge, of course!' "

I laughed, for Peter had mimicked poor advocate Craigsdale perfectly.

"Andrea," Peter said darkly, ignoring my laugh, "I happen to know that the Earl of Devbridge is in his fifties, if he's a day, and has two sons, one my age." His voice was earnest now as he added, "Please, Drea, say that Craigsdale made a mistake."

A knot formed in my stomach in spite of myself, and I nervously sipped at my port. Rallying, I managed to say with some spirit, "I am sorry, Peter, that you found out in this way. I had meant to tell you yesterday . . . but . . . it didn't seem the proper time," I finished lamely.

Peter rose swiftly and strode across the room and back again. He leaned over me and cupped my downcast face in his hand. "Look at me, Drea," he commanded. "I won't yell at you, for I know that you will yell back and that will solve naught. But you must tell me why. Why do you choose to marry a man more than twice your age?"

I thought frantically of a way to begin my rehearsed explanation but could not seem to recall a part of it that would answer his question.

He shook his head, perplexed. "It cannot be for position, and certainly not for money! Lord knows, you can look as high as you wish for a husband!" He paused for a moment and took a deep breath. "I know it has been difficult without Grandfather."

To my surprise, I felt tears spring to my eyes. The pain was bittersweet as I remembered that Grandfather had disapproved of tears, "succumbing to womanish vapors," he would remark acidly.

"Have you been so unhappy, little sister?" Peter asked gently.

I gave no answer, being much too occupied in trying to stop the tears that were spilling onto my cheeks.

"Come, tell me about it," he said kindly.

I gave a final watery sniff, blew my nose on Peter's

proffered handerchief, and looked up diffidently into his worried face.

I began slowly, my voice so low that Peter had to lean closer to me to hear. "When Grandfather died, I had no one to . . . to help me with my grief. You had not yet returned from the Continent. Most of my friends were so, oh, how should I say it . . . so cloyingly solicitous."

"Yes, I know," Peter interrupted, "more hair than wit. And I, too, should have been here sooner."

I said quickly, "Oh, no, Peter, don't tease yourself. I know that you came as soon as you could. In any case," I continued, "one day, about a week after Grandfather's funeral, the Earl of Devbridge sent his card. He was so kind, but he didn't make me feel like, you know, a weak, helpless female. He seemed to understand how I felt, but he didn't make me sad or uncomfortable. We talked of Grandfather, for even though Grandfather had been some years his senior, they had been friends. Evidently Grandfather had made his entry into the ton easier by sponsoring him at White's and the Four Horsemen's Club."

Peter frowned. "I never heard Grandfather mention the Earl of Devbridge before. Doesn't that seem rather strange to you, Drea?"

I nodded. "Yes, it did, and so I asked the earl why we had never met before. He said that after Grandfather married and retired to Yorkshire they had lost track of each other."

Peter looked unconvinced, but motioned for me to continue.

I took a deep breath and said anxiously, "Peter, please try to understand. You know I am not a lightweight schoolgirl. Why, I cut my eyeteeth years ago! And," I finished quickly, a hint of defiance in my voice, "I feel that . . . Lawrence can offer me the kind of life I want and need."

Peter rounded on me. "Drea, that is no answer, no answer at all! Dammit it, sister, what is it you want and need—another grandfather?"

My temper flared in spite of my intentions. "That was totally uncalled for," I cried angrily. "What do you know of my wants and needs? You who travel, at whim, unhampered by petticoats and polite society's strictures?"

"What would you, sister, model yourself after that Stanhope woman who travels the world in trousers and consorts with evil-smelling bedouins? Come," he rapped contemptuously, "that is nonsense and you well know it!"

I responded coldly, bring the argument around again to where it belonged. "Marriage is not part of that 'nonsense,' as you put it. It appears that I have come around to your way of thinking."

"Yes, evidently you have. But this solution is not one whit better. And that brings us back to the earl, does it not?"

"Yes, I suppose it does."

There was an uncomfortable silence. Peter sat back, twirling his empty glass, and looked at me meditatively. "Tell me, Drea, do you love him?"

I was taken off guard by his question and laughed uncertainly. "Really, Peter, what a thing to ask!" I rose quickly and walked across the room, my back to my brother. He must stop this line of questioning, I thought frantically, for I knew that I could not lie to him.

He continued in the same meditative voice, as if he were talking to himself, "Devbridge, from what I hear, is pretty plump in the pocket himself, so I believe we can safely assume that he is no fortune hunter."

I whirled around at him, my eyes staring daggers.

He met my gaze impassively, and said with deadly calm, "You will not tell me that you are in love with him, so I am forced to conclude what I originally said—

you, my dear sister, need and want another aged mentor! I was unaware that the earl in any way resembles our martinet of a grandpapa. Does he?"

"Are you quite through?" I demanded, white with fury. "You've no right, Peter, no right to speak to me in that way!"

All my rehearsed conciliatory speeches were gone from my mind. Long-buried bitter words came tumbling out. "At least in this marriage, brother, I shall be spared the moritification of seeing my husband make love to the servants! I shall be spared the humiliation of watching my husband indiscriminately spread his favors among all my friends!" I was trembling uncontrollably and grasped the back of the sofa for support.

Peter looked at me for one long moment and whistled softly to himself. "I've often wondered how much you knew of our illustrious sire's . . . ah . . . amorous exploits. I had hoped that Mother would have had the good sense and intelligence to keep her bitterness to herself. But I see she did not. Poor woman," he added thoughtfully, "she was always too busy having the vapors to take time to think."

"Don't you dare talk about Mother like that," I cried. "You don't know, you cannot know what she suffered! Father killed her! She could bear no more humiliation, and—"

"And," Peter finished for me, "she caught a chill and died only a week after reaching Grandfather. Ancient history, my dear, it has nothing to do with you . . . or me."

"I would not have run away, I would have killed him!" I cried, my hands clenched into fists.

Peter answered smoothly. "How very dramatic of you, Drea."

"Well, I would have, do you hear me, Peter? He deserved to die. And if you think I would ever take a chance of that happening to me, well . . . I would rather die first!"

"Phew," Peter whistled. He stood up in front of me and pulled my hands from my burning cheeks. "Listen to me," he commanded, shaking me none too gently. "You cannot let our parents' blunders ruin your life. You think to escape our mother's humiliation by marrying a man too old to have desires . . . or unable," he added under his breath. "It is no life for you, Drea. In fact, I find the thought disgusting—you warming an old man's bed!"

I answered quickly, too quickly. "There is to be none of that!" I drew back, appalled at what I had revealed.

Peter himself took a step back, astonishment written on his face. "Oh, my God . . . now I begin to understand. I wondered why you turned down young Viscount Barresford, an excellent man and sincerely attached to you. And poor Oliver Trever—you whistled him down the wind without a thought! My God, Andrea, do you hope to avoid all unhappiness by running from life . . . by shackling yourself to an old man?"

I was silent, for I felt stripped, my most private feelings bared. Numbly I walked to the windows, my back to my brother. It seemed to me now that there was nothing I could say or do to reconcile him to my marriage.

In a stiff, contracted voice I heard myself say. "The wedding is Tuesday next. We leave immediately for Devbridge Manor. You are, of course, welcome to come . . . if you wish."

"You're a fool, Andrea," he said almost tonelessly.

I did not reply, for my throat was choked with tears.

I heard him stride quickly from the library, the doors banging behind him. Through the windows I saw Williams, the groom, bring around Peter's mare. He swung a leg over the saddle and was gone a few minutes later.

I curled up in the window seat and stared out at the gathering fog. Peter's final words rang in my head. "You're a fool, Andrea." *A fool.* Was he right? Was I escaping life, afraid of repeating my parents' failure? I dashed my hand across my eyes, trying to rub away the tears.

There was a light tap on the door, and Thorpe entered the library to announce the Earl of Devbridge. I blinked in rapid succession to make the tears recede, and I felt a flush spread over my face. Rising from the window seat, I quickly smoothed my gown and my hair.

"Andrea," he said in his well-modulated voice, "Andrea . . ."

I jumped, startled, and looked quickly around me. I was not in Grandfather's library in Cavendish Square, but rather sitting across from my husband in a gently swaying chaise.

"Andrea," he repeated, "have you been woolgathering, my dear? How ungallant of me to doze in such charming company!"

"I was just thinking of . . . P-Peter," I stammered, banishing the last uncertain questions from my mind. Lawrence leaned over and patted my gloved hands. "I know it is difficult for you. I, too, was very disappointed when Peter refused our invitation. Ah, well, he will get over his sullens, my dear. You will see."

Lawrence settled back again against the comfortable upholstered cushions and stretched his legs diagonally away from me. He folded his arms gracefully across his chest and tilted his head slightly to one side, resting his chin lightly on his cravat. I looked at him wryly, wondering how he could be so calm, so relaxed. As for myself, I was much too excited from all the newness this day had brought to think of dozing! I looked out of the window, hoping to get a better view of the countryside, and was surprised at the sudden darkness of the afternoon. It began to drizzle, and I pulled the warm rug snugly about my legs. The chaise was well-sprung and quite luxurious, I thought, as I fingered the pale blue satin upholstery. I removed a lemon kid glove so that I could touch the soft fabric, and in doing so, revealed the Devbridge family ring that encircled my finger. I gazed at the massive ring, and realized with a start that I was now the Countess of Devbridge.

Toward evening we arrived in Repford, where Lawrence had arranged accommodations for us at the White Hart Inn. No sooner had we bowled into the yard than several boys came running to hold the horses and open the chaise door.

We were greeted at the door with a very low bow from our landlord.

"Good day, Pratt," Lawrence greeted. "I trust our accommodations are ready?"

"Yes, indeed, my lord, if your lordship and ladyship will accompany me, I will show you to your private parlour."

Pratt beamed when I delighted in the cozy, wood-paneled room. I tossed my muff on a chair, walked over to the bright fire, and fanned my hands toward the blaze. Lawrence gave orders for our supper. When Pratt had bowed himself out, Lawrence joined me by the fire.

"I think the good Pratt could vie with our royal dukes in the nobility of his bow," I commented lightly.

"True. But you should not poke fun at the locals, my dear." Lawrence smiled wryly.

When Pratt came again into the parlour, he was followed by a large smiling girl whose name, we were informed, was Betty.

Lawrence turned to me. "Would half an hour suit you, Andrea, before we dine?"

"Quite generous." I smiled and followed Betty from the room. Once in my room, I dismissed her quickly, for I wished to be alone. I set the branch of candles close to the mirror and began to brush out my crumpled hair. My face was pale and shadowy in the soft candlelight. For a moment I felt suddenly very alone, very vulnerable; but it passed quickly, for I was used to being my own mistress and by myself. Except, of course, for Grandfather. I frowned away the unhappiness and cheered myself with Lady Fremont's words at the Camerleighs' ball. "What a sly puss you are, Andrea Jameson," she said, tapping her fan on my arm. "Here you have trapped one of the most eligible men in England, and right under the noses of all those scheming mamas!"

The polite world thought I had made a good match, and so did I. Only Peter did not. I sighed, picked up the branch of candles, gave my hair a final pat, and walked downstairs. The parlour was filled with delectable smells. Lawrence sat by the fire reading a newspaper, and Pratt was busy crowding our table with roast mutton, a raised pie, a brace of partridge, and innumerable side dishes.

I was ravenously hungry and partook liberally of every dish that was passed to me. I had just ladled another portion of a delicious fish stew when I glanced up at Lawrence. He was looking in some astonishment at my refilled plate. I stopped, my spoon in midair. "I am positively famished, and our good Pratt does serve a wonderful fish stew," I said somewhat defensively.

Lawrence grimaced and then sighed. "I do not mean to embarrass you, my dear. I momentarily forgot the extraordinary appetites of the young."

I laughed and retorted, "Ah, but I am now a married lady, my dear sir, and can no longer by considered in the ranks of the young. Why, I assure you, I am beginning to feel positively matronly!"

Lawrence stiffened. The laughter died on my lips. I had meant no insult, no slight to his age. I shook my head in denial and began to stammer out an explanation, when Lawrence interrupted. "No, my dear, do not apologize. It has been a fatiguing day and we both are tired. Of course you meant no harm."

I wasn't the least bit tired, but I wisely refrained from saying so. I lowered my head and continued with my fish stew.

When Pratt again appeared with the smiling Betty to remove the covers, he poured Lawrence a glass of port. Lawrence raised the glass to his lips and nodded his approval. Unthinking, I held up my glass. A lady desiring a gentleman's drink somewhat discomfited the poor Pratt. His eyes appealed to my husband for guidance. Lawrence's face remained impassive and he merely indicated with a nod that Pratt fill my glass. I smiled to myself, remembering my grimaces when I first tasted port. Grandfather had chided, "It's part of your education. You ain't going to be a simpering miss, my girl. Drink up!"

For three years I had been admitted to that male tradition of good drinking and men's talk after dinner. Now it seemed unlikely that the earl would applaud my grandfather's indulgence. As soon as Pratt and Betty left the parlour, my husband sat back, his glass of port gracefully held between slender fingers, and regarded me gravely. I was hesitant to speak, for fear of again offending. I sat, miserably silent, waiting to be given a setdown. It was not long in coming.

He said coldly and precisely, "I presume the duke is responsible for your, ah, somewhat unusual taste in drink."

I prepared to defend Grandfather, when Lawrence interposed, "I must admit to surprise and some dismay, Andrea, but I am certainly not unreasonable, nor an ogre. Let us say that you may continue your drinking habits, but only when we are alone. Do you agree?"

"You make it sound as if I were some sort of loose, immoral creature," I muttered stiffly.

He laughed lightly, breaking the tension. "I am truly sorry, my dear. I do not mean to scold. But I must insist that it remain our secret."

As I continued to look mutinous, he coaxed, "Whatever would the polite world say if they knew that the Countess of Devbridge imbibed port after dinner with the gentlemen!"

I was obliged to agree with his observation, but I still felt compelled to defend Grandfather and myself. I embarked on a disjointed attempt at justification, when Lawrence, looking faintly amused, cut me off. "Enough! Let us drink to the new Countess of Devbridge!" The corners of my mouth lifted, and I raised my glass to his.

We soon adjourned from the table to the fire. "Lawrence," I began, making myself comfortable in a winged chair beside the warm blaze, "since I am now in the Devbridge family, it is time that you told me more about my new family, the manor, and, of course, about the family skeletons," I added, a twinkle in my eyes.

"That is much too long a recital to begin this evening," he protested, stretching his elegantly clad legs toward the fire. "We have a long day tomorrow and there will be ample time to bore you with details of my family . . . and its skeletons." So saying, he stretched and rose slowly, holding out his hand to help me rise.

I felt somewhat deflated at being so peremptorily dismissed to bed, for there was much I wished to know.

I reluctantly rose and took his hand. He walked me to my bedchamber, smiled down at me silently for a moment, and gave me a gentle pat on the cheek. "Pleasant dreams, my dear. After the port, I have no doubt that you will sleep well." Without awaiting a reply, he turned and left me.

After a light breakfast the next morning, we emerged from the inn, only to find that the weather was still gray and damp. "Most unusual," Lawrence commented when I jested that I felt myself back in the North Country.

Lawrence was quiet this morning, as if he were preoccupied with some important matter. I hoped that it concerned estate matters and not my introduction to his family. Perhaps, I reasoned, he was simply bored with the long trip, as was I.

Occasionally he broke our silence by pointing in the general direction of landmarks of interest, but the gray mist formed an impenetrable veil, shrouding the countryside.

As the day wore on, my apprehension grew, for I knew that we were expected for dinner. "If we are late, will your family wait dinner for us?" I asked, finally broaching the subject of his family.

He looked up, startled. "What a question! Of course they will. But don't fret, we shall arrive in good time." He again lapsed into silence. I eyed him uncertainly for a moment and then decided that my agitation was more important than his silent thoughts.

"Lawrence, could you not tell me more about Devbridge Manor, and, of course, about my new family?"

He looked up again, his face losing his abstracted gaze, and said contritely, "Forgive my inattention, Andrea. Today was my turn for woolgathering."

"'Tis not important," I assured him. I added in a more serious voice, "I really know far too little about the Devbridge family, Lawrence, including your two sons."

"That is true. Shall I take the chance of boring you with the antiquity of Devbridge Manor?"

"On the contrary, sir, how could I possibly be bored with what is now my own family?" I responded truthfully.

This seemed to please him, for he began to speak

warmly. "Well, then, let me begin at the beginning. That would be the esteemed Hugo, the first Earl of Devbridge. Good Queen Bess gave him the title in 1585, I think. Let us say that Queen Elizabeth rewarded him for his indefatigable efforts at establishing the true faith in England."

My face looked a question.

"Indeed," Lawrence responded to my silent inquiry, "I fear that the estimable Hugo was something of a religious fanatic. It seems that he was continually contriving to blot out the 'heretical blight that infests our fair land,' as he put it in his diary, if my memory serves me correctly."

"His diary still exists?" I asked, eyes alight.

"Parts of it. The pages that remain are under glass in the Old Hall. I will show them to you. But, to continue."

"Hugo," I prompted.

"Ah, yes. As I said, Hugo was rewarded for his diligence. With the title, the queen also bestowed upon him and his heirs some very rich lands and an annuity. Hugo began building immediately and Devbridge Manor was completed toward 1590. Have I succeeded in boring you?"

"Certainly not. Please continue," I responded.

He looked thoughtful for a moment. "Let me see. The succeeding earls flourished under the Stuarts, being stout royalists. Unfortunately, this proved to be their undoing, for Cromwell and his Roundheads took the manor when James, then earl, and a most unsteady fellow, from what I have read, was hosting a regiment of royalist troops. Most of the manor was destroyed during the fighting, and only the Old Hall remains intact today."

"Goodness gracious," I exclaimed. "What happened to James?"

"He followed the king and went to the executioner's

block," Lawrence said, giving his neck a light chop with his hand.

"Ugh," I grimaced.

"A good thing for the Devbridge line that the Stuarts came back quickly. From then until now, we have flourished. My most immediate ancestors managed to please their most Germanic highnesses and have been duly rewarded. And that, my dear, brings us to today."

"And the manor itself, when was it rebuilt, Lawrence?"

"As I said, the Old Hall remains from Tudor times. Every Devbridge since then has added his own particular artistic notions, and the manor today is a somewhat ungainly mixture of architectural styles."

I laughed. "Will I get lost in long, musty hallways?"

"It will take you a while to learn your way around," he admitted, "but we've closed off the north wing, so there will be fewer dark, musty corridors for you to worry about." Although his voice was light, I could sense his obvious pride.

"Sir, I admit readily to being impressed with your lineage, for your title and lands precede my own by a good hundred years," I teased. "Why, Deerfield Hall is a modern upstart compared to Devbridge Manor. But to continue. Tell me more about my new family." The past history of Devbridge Manor did not greatly concern me. But his family was quite another matter. I tensed, thinking about the possible reception I might receive from his two sons.

Lawrence, of course, sensed my trepidation. He leaned over and possessed himself of my gloved hands and said gently, "Do not be nervous, Andrea, everyone will be delighted with you."

"Even your two sons?" I asked.

"Yes, even my two sons," he responded firmly. "The younger, Thomas, is a careful fellow. You will probably find him something of a slowtop. But he is a good son and has cared for the estate since he returned from Oxford. His wife, Amelia—she was Colonel Blandeston's girl . . ."

I shook my head, for I did not recognize the name.

"It is no wonder you do not know her, for she and Thomas were not in London for the Season last year. 'Tis a pity, for Amelia is a social creature and pines for London with all its routs and balls. Unfortunately, Thomas contracted an inflammation of the lung that laid him up for quite some months, and they were unable to go."

"Is he well now?" I inquired politely.

"Oh, yes. But as I said, he is a careful fellow, and his health is of great importance to him."

"Do Thomas and Amelia have children?" I could not bring myself to ask Lawrence if he had grandchildren.

"Not yet, but of course we're hoping." Lawrence was silent for a moment.

"And your elder son?" I prompted.

"Ah, yes, John . . . my heir."

I looked at him sharply. I sensed a tension in his voice, some sort of strong emotion. I wondered if perhaps it was not bitterness. Lawrence obviously, in any case, did not wish to speak of John. What had John done? I wondered.

To my surprise, Lawrence spoke in a quite flat, ordinary voice. "John has not been much with us in recent years. He has traveled the Continent since he left Oxford eight years ago. He just recently sold out, resigned his commission. I trust he is ready to undertake his duties now."

In spite of Lawrence's obvious reserve about his son, I could not resist asking, "Was he at Waterloo, sir?"

"Yes, indeed," came his stiff reply. "A wounded hero. That brought him home three months to recuperate from the ball in his shoulder. But then he was off again."

"Do you think he knows Peter?" I asked excitedly.

"I would consider it likely." His face was closed, and so, I assumed, was our conversation about John. I had more questions but held my tongue. I hoped that perhaps the rift between Lawrence and John would mend now that John had returned home.

The gray afternoon dissolved into a dark, damp evening. I was feeling increasingly restive and anxious for the journey to end. Lawrence leaned toward the window and said with pride, "We're coming into the park now. Soon you will see the manor."

My first response to Devbridge Manor was something akin to awe, for as we swept around a curve, it stood like a vast, rambling monolith before us. In the vastness were points of light, giving the entire structure an eerie quality. Four towers, circular and tall, stood at the corners of the manor like great sentinels. From what I could make out in the darkness, the towers were like the fists of long arms that stretched out in four directions from the center.

As our steaming horses came to a halt before the manor, a footman opened the doors to the chaise and helped me down gently. He raised an umbrella quickly over my head.

"Welcome home, milord," came a rich, deep voice.

"It is good to be home, thank you, Bates," Lawrence said as he climbed out after me.

I walked carefully up well-worn stone steps to the great front doors. They were flung open by another footman, who bowed deeply as we passed. The entranceway was softly lit by flambeaux fastened to the stone walls. Their glowing light played softly on the old and faded tapestries that were hanging between them.

"Welcome home, my lord, my lady," said a very imposing man, who bowed to Lawrence and me. He gestured to the footman, who deftly removed our outer cloaks.

Lawrence said, "I hope all is well, Brantley."

"Yes, my lord."

"Brantley, this, of course, is your new mistress." Again, Brantley, who I assumed was the family butler, executed a marvelous bow. He seemed pleased in a very restrained way and maintained a steady flow of conversation with Lawrence as he led us down the hallway.

Brantley threw open another set of doors, and said in awe-inspiring tones, "The Earl and Countess of Devbridge."

The drawing room was long and narrow with a high-vaulted ceiling. Dark red hangings and furnishings dominated the room, and a myriad of candles burned brightly.

There were three people in the room with startled expressions on their faces.

TWO

My husband gave my arm a reassuring squeeze and said, "I am glad you are all here. Thomas, Amelia, John, I would like you to meet Andrea . . . my wife." There was a brief moment of silence until the younger of the two men hastened forward. The woman rose somewhat reluctantly and followed him slowly. The other man—I assumed it was John—remained leaning easily against the mantel, gazing impassively at us.

"Father, I am glad you're home," Thomas said, grasping his father's hand in welcome.

"Andrea, this is my son Thomas, and Amelia, his wife," Lawrence said, smiling.

"Delighted to meet you, Andrea," Thomas said, and shook my hand warmly. As I looked up at him, I smiled, for he was obviously his father's son. Both were slender and of medium height and carried themselves with a kind of quiet assurance. Thomas' pale blue eyes were warm, and crinkled at the corners when his mouth smiled. I could not help but feel that he was genuinely pleased to meet me.

"Father, you have been away too long," Amelia chided as she brushed her lips against his cheek. She kept her head resolutely turned from me, as if she did not wish to acknowledge my presence.

"It is good to be back, Amelia," Lawrence replied, giving her a gentle hug. "Now, my dear," he said firmly, "you will want to meet Andrea."

I responded instantly and stretched out my hand to her. "I have heard much of you, Amelia. I am very pleased to meet you."

"Charmed, I'm sure," she responded vaguely, and lightly touched my hand. She looked down at me appraisingly, and at that moment I bitterly resented my lack of inches. She was a regally tall and lovely woman of perhaps twenty-seven or -eight. Her hair was black as a raven's wing and drawn up into a knot of loose curls; her eyes were a rich brown set beneath perfectly arched black brows. I looked back to Thomas as he announced gaily, "Father, look who has arrived—our prodigal John!"

I looked beyond Thomas to John. He had still not come forward, but now his eyes met his father's.

"Well, John, it is good you are home . . . at last," Lawrence said evenly. I looked up quickly at my husband, for there was no warmth in his voice. He seemed to stiffen slightly as John strode over to us, his eyes never leaving his father's face. Like Thomas, he was dressed in evening attire, but there all similarity ended. He was a tall and a powerfully built man who towered over Thomas and his father. His face was deeply tanned from his years of campaigning, and his hair, like Amelia's, was raven black. His eyes were so dark that they appeared black in the soft lighting, and his brows were thick and slightly arched. His face was set into an impassive mask, as if he were controlling some violent emotion. I frowned slightly, for he looked cold and aloof, so different from his smiling brother, Thomas.

He took his father's hand and said briefly, "As you see, Father, I have come home to assume my filial duties."

Lawrence slowly took his son's outstretched hand and answered shortly, "Yes, John, so I see. We will hope that this time you will stay with us."

John turned in my direction and made a slight ironical bow. He said in an indifferent, drawling voice, "What a singularly pleasant surprise . . . er . . . ma'am."

"Andrea," snapped Lawrence.

"Ah, yes . . . Andrea," he repeated in the same drawling tone. He leaned forward and lazily took my hand in his and drew it to his lips. I felt a flush of anger at his flippancy, and thrust up my chin, looking squarely into his dark eyes. "An equally . . . pleasant surprise to make your acquaintance . . . sir," I said, trying to match his indifferent tone. A black eyebrow rose, and he looked faintly amused. At least he could not think me poor-spirited, I thought, returning a cold stare.

Again there was a moment of silence before Lawrence said to all of us in general, "I am glad you waited dinner. Amelia, my dear, will you please ring for Brantley? Andrea," he continued, looking at me, "will, say, half an hour be ample time for you to refresh yourself?"

Knowledge of my crumpled appearance won out over my hunger, and I replied promptly. "Certainly, Lawrence."

"Good. Amelia, would you please see Andrea to her room?"

Amelia hesitated for a brief moment and then nodded slowly. We started toward the door, when she stopped abruptly, turned, and inquired of Lawrence, "Mrs. Eliott has prepared the Blue Room. She seemed convinced that this was your wish. We all felt, of course, that she must be mistaken . . ." Her voice trailed off uncertainly.

Lawrence replied evenly, "There is no mistake, Amelia." He turned away from us and walked toward Thomas and John. Amelia looked puzzled and then gave a careless shrug and walked from the room. I followed in her wake silently, wondering why she had questioned my having the Blue Room. As she motioned me toward the staircase, it was on the tip of my tongue to ask her, but her face was a forbidding mask. I would find out soon enough, I thought, quickening my pace to accommodate her long stride.

The staircase curved down into the center of what had to be the Old Hall, the only original part of the manor to survive. It was of noble proportions, with a tall wooden-beamed, smoke-blackened ceiling, barely visible in the dim light. One wall was dominated by a gigantic fireplace that resembled a great blackened cavern in the half-light. The stone floor was bare and echoed strangely as Amelia's shoes click-clacked on her way to the staircase. Thick carpeting covered the exquisitely carved staircase, which could accommodate four people side by side. Branches of candles lit our way up the winding stairs. When we reached the landing, I turned to gaze down at the Old Hall. It seemed part of another place and time, a relic, but with a certain dignity that would be ageless.

My thoughts were interrupted by Amelia, who began in a contemptuous voice, "Of course, you have never been in such a house as this."

I looked up at her quickly, not at first understanding her implied insult, for a headache was beginning to nag at me, and I thought that perhaps I had not heard her properly. "I beg your pardon?" I asked carefully.

She paused for a moment and then sniffed disdainfully. "What I meant was that when people are first presented to surroundings such as this"—she indicated the Old Hall with an eloquent wave of her arm—"they tend to be . . . overcome. It is to be expected."

I was taken aback by this direct attack, and my temper flared. But I was determined not to respond to her in kind. Instead, I replied with tolerable calm, "I assure you, Amelia, that if I were not beset with fatigue and hunger, I would go into positive raptures over the antiquity of this establishment."

As she continued to eye me with considerable hostility, I added briefly, "When I am rested, I assure you that I shall be properly effusive, as people are, I understand . . . in the country."

She drew an audible breath, and her black brows arched up in surprise at my retort, for if nothing else, she could not put me down as a tongue-tied miss. She looked a trifle disconcerted as she turned quickly on her heel and walked down the hallway to the right.

I took a deep breath and followed after her. We passed door after door, until she finally stopped at the end of the corridor. There were two doors here, and as she opened them, she announced dramatically, "This is the Blue Room." It was now my turn to arch my brows in surprise.

My first impression was that I had suddenly been immersed in the bluest of seas. Varying shades of blue coverings hung from the walls, and the carpeting was a pale blue, thick and warm. The bed was set on a dais with dark blue hangings. Arranged charmingly in front of the fireplace was a sitting area, all the furniture in blues and delicate beiges. The effect was like being in a fragile, elaborate fairy kingdom below the sea.

"It is truly beautiful," I breathed. Impulsively I turned to Amelia and asked, "Why was there some question about my having this room?"

She looked momentarily startled, and then a guarded

expression appeared in her eyes. She answered repressively, "Oh, nothing, really."

I was about to pursue my questioning when we were interrupted by a light knock on the door.

"Come in," said Amelia sharply, obviously relieved.

A pretty young maid stood hesitantly in the doorway.

"Well, stop gawking and come over here, girl," Amelia commanded, beckoning to the maid with an impatient hand.

I smiled at the maid reassuringly.

"Belinda," Amelia said in the way of an introduction, "this is your new mistress . . . the Countess of Devbridge." She seemed all at once surprised and upset that this was indeed my new position.

Belinda bobbed a graceful curtsy and smiled at me shyly.

"I am glad to meet you, Belinda," I said warmly. "I am certain we shall deal together quite well."

Amelia said brusquely, "I shall leave you now. Belinda will look after you, until, of course, your own personal maid arrives . . . if you have one." She sniffed.

"No, I do not," I replied wearily, not wishing to bait her further.

Amelia turned and left the room. I gave a small sigh of relief and turned my attention to Belinda. I judged her to be about my age or perhaps a year or two younger. She had lovely chestnut hair topped by a charming little cap, and a trim little figure. Remembering that I now had less than half an hour, I said quickly, "Well, Belinda, we have only a short time to render me presentable for dinner."

She cocked her head to one side and said cheerfully, "We'll have you right as rain in no time at all, my lady."

As she spoke, she began helping me out of my gray traveling gown. When I was undressed to my shift, Belinda gestured to a basin of water on the commode.

"While your ladyship bathes, I can unpack a gown," she said briskly.

The headache had developed into a steady pounding at my temples. I had to gather my wits and give her instructions. "I'll wear the pale blue velvet gown . . . it's in the large trunk, over there."

A short time later I was dressed and Belinda had deftly arranged my hair in an elegant style on top of my head. " 'Tis like spun gold my lady, so beautiful and thick," she commented as she vigorously brushed the side curls into obedience. A bit of powder and the matched pearls Lawrence had given me as a wedding present, and Belinda deemed me presentable. She twitched a final pleat into place and stood back proudly to let me pass.

A footman appeared in the corridor and escorted me back to the drawing room. As I entered, I was again aware of startled glances. It was then that I realized how my earlier appearance must have made me appear to them. In my high-necked, demure gray gown, hair in disarray, I must have looked like a dowdy schoolgirl.

Lawrence came forward and possessed himself of my hand. "You look charmingly, my dear." He added with gentle mockery, glancing at his watch, "And not so late that dinner is quite cold."

I happened to look up at John, to see him gaze in some surprise at his father.

"I've ordered dinner to be laid in the morning room," Lawrence commented as we passed from the Old Hall into another brightly lit corridor toward the back of the manor. "The formal dining room seats forty or so guests, and we would, I fear, be shouting rather than conversing."

Brantley opened a door, and Lawrence ushered me into a small but elegantly furnished dining room. He helped me into my chair at the foot of the table. As he seated himself at the head of the table, he looked up, as did I, to see Amelia hesitate by my place. I cast an anxious glance at Lawrence and began, "Perhaps it would be better if . . ." Lawrence shook his head at me and said smoothly, "Andrea, you are now mistress of the house. Amelia, my dear, come and sit on my right."

Amelia flushed slightly and gave her now-familiar shrug, allowing a footman to seat her.

The first course was set in front of me, but my appetite was rapidly disappearing, for my head was beginning to pound unbearably. I was grateful that Thomas relieved me of the need to converse when, in his easy way, he began to describe estate matters to his father.

"John has learned a great deal since returning, Father. You remember how all the tenants were forever praising him." He sounded genuinely pleased, and I wondered fleetingly how he could be, considering that he himself had been filling John's position for several years. He was either sincere or an excellent actor, I decided.

Lawrence looked questioningly at John. "Is this true, John? Have you really decided to stay this time and help manage the estate?"

"Indeed yes, Father," John replied. "Thomas can vouch for me—I've been a willing and faithful student. Isn't that so, brother?" he asked, turning to Thomas.

"He's applied himself admirably, Father, I assure you," Thomas said gaily.

Lawrence looked thoughtfully at John and merely nodded in seeming approval. He then turned to Amelia, who to this point had been silently picking at her food, her head down. "And what of you, my dear? What have you been about in my absence?"

She slowly raised her head and forced a smile. "Nothing in particular, Father, just my usual pursuits."

I wondered what her usual pursuits might be but decided that an inquiry from me would not be warmly received.

"Well, now that we are all together again, there will be much to keep us all pleasantly occupied," Lawrence pronounced, unperturbed.

The conversation lagged through several more interminable courses. When Brantley finally entered bearing port for the men, I felt an undeniable surge of relief. Lawrence must have noticed me gazing longingly at the decanter, for his eyes twinkled with suppressed mirth and he said hurriedly, "My dear, I promise that we will join you shortly."

I smiled only faintly, for he did not realize that I wished the port to dull my headache.

A footman drew back my chair for me to rise. Amelia rose very slowly, and I was forced to wait for her at the door. She said nothing as we crossed back to the drawing room.

As I seated myself close to the fire, I decided to make another effort, and ventured tentatively, "The furnishings are very tasteful, Amelia. I'll wager you are responsible."

"Indeed," came the clipped reply. She added nothing further, and sat gazing fixedly into the fire.

Very well, I thought, even if she continues to snub me, I shall not be provoked. I leaned back in my chair and closed my eyes, hoping this would lessen the pounding in my head.

The silence remained unbroken for several minutes. At last Amelia began in a honey-sweet voice, "Is your . . . er . . . family in London?"

Ah, here we go again, I thought, wincing. Determined not to rise to the bait and further ruffle her, I answered in a sincere voice, "No, as a matter of fact, they are not." I started to add that I had no family save one brother, when she interrupted me with more words cloaked in honeyed tones. "I do hope that the earl was fortunate enough to have the opportunity of meeting your . . . ah . . . family before your marriage."

I grinned to myself in spite of my headache at this blatant assault from Amelia. Obviously she thought I was an adventuress, a fortune hunter! I remarked cordially, "Oh, yes, indeed, Lawrence was granted the opportunity of meeting my family. Unfortunately, I had to forgo the privilege of meeting his until after the wedding."

I heard a sharp intake of breath. Any reply that she might have made was forestalled by the entrance of the gentlemen. Thomas crossed over to Amelia and asked in his jovial voice. "I hope you and Andrea have been getting better acquainted, my love."

Poor Thomas, I thought, how little you know of the matter!

Amelia looked the picture of innocent bewilderment and responded in an injured tone, "I was wishing to talk to Andrea about her family, but she seems strangely reluctant . . ." Her statement hung suspended, and I saw her give John a conspiratorial grin. Indeed, I thought angrily, this is going too far!

Before I could respond, Lawrence turned to Amelia and said gently, "Andrea's natural modesty undoubtedly prevented her. She would not want to be thought unbecomingly forward."

I looked up at him, blinking rapidly, wondering what kind of game he was playing. Everyone was gazing at him expectantly, waiting for him to continue.

Lawrence appeared to be enjoying himself immensely. Finally Thomas asked impatiently, "Come, Father, why would Andrea appear forward?"

Lawrence said blandly, "I am sure all of you remember Oliver Fortescue." Amelia frowned. "The Duke of Watford," Lawrence continued smoothly. "He was Andrea's grandfather. He owned vast estates near York, and a fine Yorkshireman he was." His voice sounded genuinely regretful. "I assume, Andrea," he asked, turning to me, "that Peter has inherited the estates?"

"Certainly a large part of them," I replied, "but there is a male cousin who now bears the title."

John turned abruptly to me, his brows raised in surprise. "Peter . . . Captain Peter Jameson . . . he's your brother?"

"Why, yes. Do you know him, John?"

"Yes, indeed, we served together in several campaigns. There is a great likeness. I should have recognized you sooner." The lazy, bored drawl was gone as he continued, now quite animated, "Peter used to speak about his madcap little sister who was always getting into scrapes."

I flushed. "Peter is forever exaggerating," I said hastily.

"Is Peter in London?" John continued.

"No," I replied. "He left last week to join Lord Brooke's staff in Brussels. I do not expect him to return for another six months."

"I shall look forward to seeing Peter again." John turned to Amelia and asked, "You remember Peter Jameson, don't you, Amelia? We were two raw young bucks, very unpolished young gentlemen. Wasn't it during your first Season?"

"My dear John," she replied coolly, "I am unable to recall every raw young buck, as you so quaintly put it. There were so many, after all."

Thomas interjected enthusiastically, "By Jove, I remember him! Always ready for a lark, wasn't he, John?"

John grinned his answer.

"Why, I remember—" Thomas began.

Lawrence interrupted Thomas' reminiscences, saying, "Now that we have settled family histories, you will be able to spend many hours recalling your . . . larks. But for tonight," he continued, turning to me, "it is enough. You're looking peaked, my dear. It has been a long day. Do you wish to be excused now?"

I was torn. Although my head was aching abominably, I hated to leave when it seemed that we were all getting along. Thomas made the decision for me by saying kindly, "You're right, Father, she does not look quite the thing. A good night's sleep, that's what she needs," he announced.

"Yes," I replied gratefully. "I do have the headache."

I rose and curtsied slightly and said my good nights.

"I'll accompany you to your room," Lawrence said, rising. When we reached the door, he turned and said, "I'll be back shortly."

As I looked back, I saw with some confusion that John was regarding me with a pronounced scowl on his face. I looked at him searchingly for a moment, wondering what I had done. I remained perplexed as Lawrence took my arm and steered me from the room.

"Well, Andrea, what do you think of your new home?" he asked as we ascended the stairs.

"It is truly magnificent," I replied, pausing at the landing to gaze down at the Old Hall.

"It is, is it not?" he said proudly. He added, "Do not worry about my fiercely loyal children. They will grow as fond of you as I am. You will see."

I had some grave doubts on that subject but forebore to voice them. When we reached my room, I asked impulsively, "Lawrence, why was Amelia so certain that I was not to have the Blue Room?"

He appeared to consider the question quite dispassionately for a moment or two before replying in an indifferent voice, "She was mistaken, my dear, it is nothing to concern you."

Tired of being pushed off, I persevered, "But, Lawrance, Amelia was really quite firm—"

A hard voice interrupted. "I said it is nothing to concern you, Andrea." I was alarmed and quite surprised at his cold dismissal of my question. Sensing my dismay, he quickly leaned over and lightly kissed my cheek. He straightened and said gently, "Sleep well, Andrea. Tomorrow you will meet the staff and I will see that you get a grand tour of the house and park."

I looked up at him questioningly for a moment. His face was closed, as it had been in our conversation about John earlier in the day. I held my tongue and said with as much dignity as I could muster. "I shall look forward to it, Lawrence. I wish you good night, sir."

Belinda had laid out my nightgown, and as she unbuttoned my dress, she scolded, "Your ladyship looks worn to a bone, staying up so late after your long journey. 'Tis a disgrace!"

A knock on the door brought her monologue to a halt. While she went to the door, I began taking the pins out of my hair. She returned shortly with a glass in her hand. "That was Jarrell, his lordship's valet, my lady. He said this is a medicine for your headache."

How kind of Lawrence, I thought, and gratefully downed the liquid. As I began to braid my hair, Belinda gave a gasp and exclaimed, "Oh, no, my lady, you must not braid your hair! My ma taught me that hair's alive and needs to breathe, just like we do. And," she finished, clinching the matter, "braiding cuts off the breath."

I laughed aloud, amused by this quaint bit of country wisdom. "Very well, Belinda, but you must brush out the tangles in the morning. And I warn you, I am a violent sleeper!"

When I was tucked into bed, Belinda began to draw the curtains. "No, Belinda, I never sleep with the curtains drawn," I said firmly.

She looked at me aghast. I repeated, my voice coaxing, "I am just like my hair . . . I must also get to breathe at night, and I find that impossible with the bed curtains drawn."

She sniffed, but raised no further demur.

When I was finally alone and in darkness, I stretched luxuriously in the soft covers. Already the draught was beginning to take effect. I soon fell into a sound and dreamless sleep.

Just as Belinda had predicted, I awoke feeling right as rain. I sat up, pulled the covers close about my neck, and looked about me. The Blue Room was lovely in the morning light. The curtains were partially drawn, and bright sunlight poured in. In the soft candlelight of the previous night, the different shades of blue had seemed to fill the room. Upon closer inspection this morning, I noticed that many shades of white and beige were blended skillfully into the furnishings and curtains. I pulled on my slippers and padded to the windows. Bright morning sunlight flooded the room as I pulled the curtains completely open. I leaned out of one of the large windows and regarded the magnificent prospect. Extending from the house for perhaps two hundred yards stretched a well-scythed lawn that blended in the distance into a wooded park. Toward the back of the manor I could make out an exquisitely laid-out garden, bordered by large well-trimmed hedges.

Despite the bright sun, a slight but chill autumn breeze penetrated my nightgown. As I straightened to turn back into the room, I felt a tug at the sleeve of my gown and then a tear. I looked down in dismay to see my sleeve caught on a jagged piece of metal attached to the outside of the window casement. Carefully I detached my sleeve from the metal. Upon closer inspection I saw that the jagged metal was buried partially in a small circular hole. There were several such holes placed at equal intervals along the outside casing. As I gazed again, puzzled, at the jagged metal that protruded from the hole, I suddenly realized the purpose. At one time this window had been barred! I looked up quickly to confirm my idea and saw identical small holes at the top of the casement. Gooseflesh rose on my arms and I felt my heart begin to pound uncomfortably. Why, in heaven's name, had this window been barred? And who could have been imprisoned here? I raced to the other windows and flung them open, only to find that all the windows were just the same.

I found myself shivering, as much from the cold as I was from my eerie discovery. I quickly closed the windows and stepped back into my room. Slowly my alarm began to recede as I realized that whoever had been imprisoned here must have belonged to the manor's long-forgotten past. How could it possibly concern me? I was still intrigued, though, and resolved to find out who the unfortunate person had been.

I walked thoughtfully back to my bed and tugged on the bell cord to summon Belinda.

THREE

I dressed carefully, choosing an elegant morning gown of French cambric with a demitrain. It was stylish, simple, and I hoped it added a few years to my age. Belinda dressed my hair more simply this morning, her deft fingers winding coils of hair into place and threading a light blue satin ribbon through the curls on top of my head. I asked her quizzingly if she could tell whether my hair had gotten sufficient air during the night.

"Oh, yes, my lady, 'tis more full of life and health today," she answered seriously.

I nearly asked her outright about the bars on the windows, but I decided upon a more subtle approach. "How long have you been in service here, Belinda?" I asked.

"'Twill be two years this spring, my lady."

I continued cautiously. "Has anyone occupied the Blue Room since you have been in service here?"

"Why, no, my lady," she answered, a questioning look on her face. "Too, 'twas the first time I had seen this

35

room, that is, the first time last night, my lady," she amended.

"Why is that, Belinda?"

"This room always be locked, my lady, that is, until yesterday. Mrs. Eliott opened it up, and Ella and Annie were fetched to dust and clean." She looked as if she were stating the obvious.

I persisted. "But, Belinda, why was the room locked up?"

"I don't know, my lady, but it always be locked since I was here." In a gesture particularly her own, she cocked her haid to one side, her face a picture of curiosity.

I shook my head and smiled reassuringly. "It is nothing, Belinda, nothing at all."

As I readied to leave the room, I thought to ask, "Is breakfast served in the morning room, as was dinner last evening?"

"Yes, my lady. Would you like me to show you there?" she asked.

"No, thank you, I remember the way."

The morning room was empty save for a servant who hovered over dishes on the sideboard. She turned quickly and curtsied as I entered. "Good morning," I said, smiling. "It looks as though you and I are the only ones about."

She nodded shyly and said primly, "If your ladyship would please to sit, I will serve your breakfast."

"Thank you, ah . . . " I answered with a question as I seated myself.

"Ella, my lady," she responded.

"Very well, Ella, you must bring me liberally of everything, for I am ravenous this morning. Has the family already breakfasted?"

"The gentlemen breakfast early, my lady, and Lady Amelia has a tray in her room near to noontime."

It appeared that I fell into the middle of these two schedules and would be breakfasting alone most of the time, I mused.

I was lavishly spreading butter and marmalade on my last piece of toast when there was a light knock on the door. I looked up to see a tall, angular woman enter. She was wearing a severely cut black silk dress that rustled as she walked gracefully over to me. Her dark hair was lightly sprinkled with gray and drawn back tightly into a bun at the nape of her neck. The look on her gaunt face reminded me forcibly of my great-aunt Henrietta when she was at the disagreeable duty of punishing one of her numerous offspring: she was tight-lipped and her high cheekbones were prominent on her pale face. I tried a tentative smile as she came to a halt and stood stiffly in front of me. She said in a precise, deep voice, "I am Mrs. Eliott, my lady, the housekeeper." After bobbing the sketchiest of curtsies, she added, "I do hope that your ladyship is through breakfasting."

Ignoring her lack of civility, I answered in a friendly voice, "Yes, certainly I am, Mrs. Eliott." I firmly banished my great-aunt's grim visage from my mind and indicated a chair beside me. "Won't you sit down, Mrs. Eliott?"

She looked momentarily taken aback, as servants were rarely asked to sit in the presence of their mistress, but then seated herself stiffly across from me. Before I could begin, she addressed me formally. "His lordship has informed me that your ladyship will undoubtedly wish to check the household accounts, and then, of course"—she hesitated perceptibly—"assume the management of the house." Though she tried to keep her voice devoid of feeling, I could sense her agitation.

Asking forgiveness for the small lie I was about to utter, I said firmly, "Mrs. Eliott, Sir Lawrence has spoken to me of your unflagging loyalty and efficient management of this establishment. As you may well imagine, I have had scant experience in running so large a household as Devbridge Manor." I paused momentarily before adding, "I have no intention of wresting the keys from you."

Her eyes widened, but I continued smoothly, "Indeed, I would be grateful if you would continue just as you have. Of course, I would like to approve the menus," I slipped in, "but other than that, I would be appreciative if you allowed me to benefit from your excellent experience. If you would be my instructress, Mrs. Eliott, I would indeed by pleased," I finished, meeting her gaze directly.

Her lashes fluttered a moment before she responded in her precise voice, "Yes, of course, my lady. And, thank you, my lady," she acknowledged after a slight pause.

I could not be certain, but I fancied that her gaunt features softened a bit. I leaned over and lightly touched her hand, saying, "I am certain we shall deal very well together."

As she rose to go, the door opened and the three gentlemen entered. Lawrence immediately cut off his conversation with Thomas and crossed over to me. "Good morning, my dear, I trust you are quite recovered," he said kindly.

"Completely," I assured him.

"Ah, Mrs. Eliott, I see you and her ladyship are getting acquainted."

"Yes, Lawrence," I interrupted hastily. "Mrs. Eliott has kindly offered to instruct me in all the household arts." My voice was filled with as much meaning as I dared to venture in Mrs. Eliott's presence.

There was a momentary twinkle in my husband's eyes, and, I thought, a look of approval, but his expression quickly became impassive. He knew that I had managed both my grandfather's establishments for nearly four years. Deerfield Hall, our estate in Yorkshire, was nearly the size of Devbridge Manor, and Grandfather also maintained a town house in Cavendish Square during the Season. I remembered quite clearly being sixteen years old and at my wits' end to be free of my chatterbox governess, Miss Brixton. I was determined that Briggie's reign was over! I had stormed into Grandfather's study and poured out all my grievances, completing my recital with a declaration that I would take over management of the household. Briggie could remain as a companion, if she wished, but not as a governess. Finally, I had added, Grandfather himself could quite readily complete my education. Grandfather at first laughed at my classroom rebellion, and as I remained mutinous, fell into one of his great rages. But this once, I was undaunted and shouted back, to the great delight of the servants. In the end, he agreed, and four very happy years had followed.

I was jerked back from my thoughts by the friendly good morning of a smiling Thomas. Did he always smile so? I wondered. I remembered Grandfather saying, "If a man always smiles, Drea, he's probably making some mischief."

"Good morning, Thomas," I returned in a friendly voice, scolding myself for my suspicions.

John nodded in my general direction but said nothing. I bristled instinctively and wondered at his coldness.

"Well, my dear, are you ready to meet the staff? They should all be assembled in the Old Hall to greet you," Lawrence said, proffering his arm.

Mrs. Eliott apologized as she hurried to the door. "Oh, I do beg your pardon, my lord, I forgot to tell her ladyship."

Lawrence waved a negligent hand. "Are you ready, Andrea?" As I rose, he added, "You look charmingly. Our people will be enchanted."

As we made our way into the Old Hall, he leaned

down and whispered, "Very diplomatic of you, my dear, and most kind." I smiled up at him, pleased that he approved my plan of action with Mrs. Eliott.

A seemingly endless group of people stood in a straight line, each dressed in his or her Sunday best. Their faces were alive with curiosity, and I could feel their scrutiny. We began with the kitchen staff, with the head cook, Mrs. Meldorson, making the introductions. I complimented her and all the kitchen staff on the fine dinner of the previous evening and repeated each name as the servants stepped forward to make their curtsy or their bow. Mrs. Eliott introduced the house staff, and again I repeated each name and uttered a friendly word here, a compliment there.

Then Lawrence took over and introduced the next servant. "This is Jarrell, my valet." Jarrell executed an elegant bow, and I remembered to thank him for bringing the medicine the previous evening. His impassive features cracked a bit to show a restrained pleasure.

Next stood a burly man with a deeply tanned face, who seemed very much out of place in a line of servants. John stepped forward and offered, "This is Ferguson, my valet."

Of course, I thought, they look as though they belong together. "Have you been long with Master John, Ferguson?" I asked.

"Yes indeed, milady. Me and Master Jack, we've been in many a campaign together." His voice boomed, filling the Old Hall.

"Ferguson was my batman for nearly seven years," John added by way of explanation.

We reached at last the stately Brantley, butler of the Devbridge family for nearly thirty-five years. He bowed low and formally to me and intoned in his dignified voice, "I and the entire staff welcome you to Devbridge

Manor, my lady. We hope that you will find everything to your satisfaction."

Greatly pleased at such a grand welcome, I thanked all the servants and expressed my certainty that Devbridge Manor was blessed in having so loyal and efficient a staff. I chanced to look up, and saw John looking at me with something akin to surprise in his face. Did he expect me to bungle under the pressure of meeting such a large staff? I thought indignantly.

As Lawrence dismissed the staff, I saw Amelia from the corner of my eye standing motionless at the top of the stairs. I wondered how long she had been standing there observing us. When the others followed my gaze and noticed her presence, she began to descend gracefully down the stairway.

"Good morning, all," she greeted, waving a languid hand and affecting a lazy drawl that was not unlike John's. "Well, I see that the servants have performed their sacred duty." Thomas started forward nervously, but Lawrence replied simply, "Very true, Amelia, and I am sure you noticed that all the servants were delighted with the new Countess of Devbridge."

Amelia's face hardened, and she walked stiff-backed into the drawing room. Thomas made a helpless gesture in our direction and hurried after her.

A frown gathered on Lawrence's brow. "Amelia must recognize that you are now mistress."

"She has long been in charge," I said. "Were I she, I would feel very much put out myself. In fact," I added, grinning, "I would probably have grand tantrums and drum my heels loudly on the floor!"

"You are right," he sighed. "It will take time, I suppose. It is just that I do not wish you to be made to feel uncomfortable in your own house."

"I shall be fine, you'll see," I said bracingly, and hurriedly changed the subject. "Lawrence, you will recall your promise to give me a tour of the house."

"Yes, indeed I did promise, and a very good idea," he agreed. "Now is a fine time, I believe," he added, taking out his watch.

John, silent to this point, interposed. "Father, have you forgotten your meeting with Melchen? I think that Brantley has already shown him to the library."

"Melchen, you say? Why, I had forgotten all about the man!" Lawrence exclaimed. "Andrea, my dear," he said contritely, "I pray you to forgive me, but I really must straighten out some business matters with our man, Melchen. It is pressing."

I replied impishly, "Ah, my dear sir, so quickly am I to be left alone, sacrificed to business concerns. 'Tis too cruel!"

Lawrence looked taken aback for a brief moment before he realized my jest. He pressed my arm and retorted, "Well, my dear, once a wife, and there is no more allure!"

"Touché, sir." I laughed, and turned to John. He shook his head. "I, too, must be unobliging, Andrea. There is a mill in the neighborhood, and I do not intend to miss it."

"I have it," Lawrence exclaimed suddenly. "Mrs. Eliott is the perfect substitute. Why, she knows this house probably better than John or Thomas. What do you think, my dear?"

"That is an excellent idea," I replied instantly. "It will provide me the opportunity to get to know her better."

A short time later, Mrs. Eliott and I began our tour of the first floor. Here I discovered a small delightful room, the Ladies' Parlour, as it was called, that opened up onto the garden at the side of the house.

The rooms on the second floor, in the west wing, were not so interesting. Mrs. Eliott opened door after door to reveal, for the most part, furniture draped in holland covers. I was distressed at the obvious disuse. "Yes," she agreed, "'tis a pity. It has been many years now since these rooms were filled with guests."

"Perhaps we can remedy the situation," I commented lightly. I made a firm resolve to myself that we must entertain as soon as possible.

At the end of the corridor, we reached my room, the Blue Room. Mrs. Eliott said simply as she walked past the doors, "And this is, of course, your ladyship's room."

I stopped and asked firmly, "Mrs. Eliott, I would like to know more about the Blue Room, if you please!"

She regarded me silently for a moment and said matter-of-factly, "This room was decorated as you see it now by the present earl's mother, Lady Aurelia. It has become . . . custom that the mistress of the house have this room." She moved away from the doors quickly and said with finality, "Would your ladyship like to see the family gallery now?"

I paused, wondering whether to persist. I decided, after a brief struggle, that my questions would better be asked of Lawrence. Yet, as I followed Mrs. Eliott to the south wing, I thought: If the Blue Room is for the mistress of the manor, then why did Amelia question my having it? And what of the windows—why had they been barred?

The family gallery, or the long gallery, as it was sometimes called, was a long, narrow room with thick, heavy curtains covering long windows on one side and scores of portraits on the other. There was a musty odor, and again the feeling of disuse.

"I would like to see Sir Hugo's portrait," I said immediately, looking around for a likely candidate. Mrs. Eliott seemed pleased that I was familiar with Sir Hugo.

She walked to a portrait near to the center of the gallery and said dramatically, "The first Earl of Devbridge!"

I disliked Sir Hugo on sight. His eyes were small and piercing and shone with a fanatical light; his lips were thin and mean, drawn tight in seeming perpetual disapproval of his fellow humans.

"Sir Hugo was a staunch supporter of the Church of England," Mrs. Eliott explained.

I felt a slight shiver. Indeed, he looked most suited to the ideals of persecution. He must have been a formidable enemy, I thought.

Mrs. Eliott moved on. "Here is the present earl as a young man, and beside him, his first countess."

Lawrence looked very much like Thomas, save that his face was stronger, more determined, his jaw and chin firm and prominent. He and his countess were bewigged, as fitted the fashion of thirty years ago. She was a haughty-looking woman with well-bred features and a look of boredom that brought her mouth down at the corners. I looked back again at Lawrence. Except for his clothing, he had not changed greatly over the years, I thought. I firmly dismissed the fleeting reflection that I could easily be his daughter.

Mrs. Eliott continued briskly, explaining the lives and histories of the Devbridge lords and ladies as she went. She was quite knowledgeable and passionately interested in the family. I listened politely, realizing that there was more to this woman than met the eye. When we finished our tour of the long gallery at last, I sank down onto a convenient chair and heaved a sigh. "Mrs. Eliott, I fear that the rest of the manor will have to wait until my feet have recovered!" I said, wiggling my toes inside the soft kid shoes.

She simply inclined her head slightly to signify agreement. "Is your ladyship ready perhaps for a light luncheon?" she inquired.

I immediately felt brighter at the thought of food. "An excellent suggestion. Let us go down at once." So saying, I pulled myself from the chair and bade my feet to move.

After my luncheon, I felt much refreshed and decided to take advantage of the warm day and stroll in the gardens. Brantley appeared in answer to my ring.

"Brantley, I have a great desire to enjoy probably what is to be one of our last summer days. Would you please advise me as to the most pleasant part of the gardens?"

"Certainly, my lady. Allow me to escort you."

As we walked, Brantley said in a proud voice, "The gardens are not, of course, in their full beauty. But I do not think that your ladyship will find them contemptible."

The gardens were indeed magnificent. The hedges were full and neatly trimmed, and the many winding footpaths intertwined and met at intervals, to be covered by rose bowers. After Brantley left me, I began to stroll down one of the paths, and mentally planted some of my favorite shrubs and flowers as I walked. After a while I sank down on one of the benches arranged along the paths and closed my eyes. The sun beat warmly down on my face. I began to feel drowsy, when I was startled back to being fully awake by a rustling noise. I opened my eyes and saw a pretty young girl of perhaps eleven or twelve standing a few feet away from me. She was small and dainty, with fair hair and wide, deep blue eyes. She stood staring at me with open curiosity.

"Hello," I said in a friendly voice. "What is your name?"

"Judith," she replied tentatively. She looked strangely familiar to me, and I frowned in concentration. Where could I have seen her before?

"My name's Andrea," I returned, holding out my hand.

"That's a funny name," came her candid child's reply. She advanced and took my proffered hand.

"Perhaps. But it is easy to say. Won't you try it?"

"Andrea," she said slowly. "It is easy to say," she pronounced.

I wondered who she could be. Certainly she was no servant's child, for her voice was well-bred and she was dressed with elegance.

"Who is your papa, Judith?" I ventured, taking the direct approach.

Again the curious stare. "My papa is the Earl of Devbridge." Her tone implied that my mental powers must be lacking, not to know so obvious a fact.

I felt surprised and somewhat shaken by this revelation. Could she be a love child, the earl's love child? I pursued, "Who is your mama, Judith?"

"Mama was papa's wife, of course." Again her voice implied that I must be a person of great ignorance. She added confidentially, "My mama's dead, actually. She died right after I was born, so I really never knew her."

My mind was in a whirl. If her mother died right after Judith's birth, she could not possibly have been Lawrence's first wife. The first countess, John and Thomas' mother, had died more than fifteen years ago! There had been, then, a second Countess of Devbridge.

"I see," I finally responded, trying to control the agitation in my voice.

"Andrea, Andrea, are you all right? You look kind of pale." There was a child's innocent concern in her voice.

I pulled myself together and managed a smile. "I am fine, Judith, just fine. I am just . . . surprised . . . and pleased to meet you."

"I am surprised too," came the forthright reply. "We've all been wondering what you would be like. I was expecting someone older . . . more like papa. You're rather young and beautiful."

"I hope you're not disappointed, Judith," I replied, somewhat shaken still, but amused at the same time.

At that moment we heard a woman's voice calling, "Judith, Judith . . . where are you, poppet?"

Very soon a tall, slender young woman appeared. "So, there you are, odious child." Her voice sounded serious, but her brown eyes twinkled.

"Gilly, Gilly," Judith said excitedly, "come and meet Andrea. She's Papa's new wife."

As she walked gracefully toward us, she said, laughing, "Ah, Judith, you must learn, poppet, to give me my full dignity . . . especially for new introductions!"

"I'm sorry, Gilly," Judith said contritely, but her eyes sparkled happily. Turning to me, she said, "Andrea, this is Miss Gillbank, my governess, and," she added in a rush, "my very best friend."

I instantly rose and held out my hand. Miss Gillbank said in a warm, pleasing voice as she took my hand, "I am very delighted to meet you, my lady. I am sure that our Judith has been telling you of our excitement!"

"Oh, yes, Judith has been telling me a lot of things," I replied, smiling down at Judith.

In mock horror Miss Gillbank said, "Oh, no, poppet, have you ruined us all?"

"Oh, Gilly," Judith laughed uncertainly and blushed.

Miss Gillbank turned back to me and said in her charming manner, "I hope the child hasn't worn you to a frazzle."

"Oh, no," I exclaimed. "I have been much entertained by such lovely company."

Miss Gillbank simply nodded, smiling. "Come, Judith, it is time for your geography lesson. We do not wish to plague her ladyship on her first day among us!"

Judith asked in an anxious voice, "You haven't been plagued, have you, Andrea?"

When I assured her that nothing of the kind had occurred, Judith clapped her hands excitedly and asked, "Would you like to see the schoolroom, Andrea? I've all sorts of maps and drawings . . . and wonderful things to show you."

"Now, poppet—" Miss Gillbank began.

"I would be delighted, dear," I interrupted. "Lead the way!"

Judith alternately skipped and ran ahead of us, looking back frequently to be sure that we followed.

Miss Gillbank shook her head and said fondly, "What a child! I do hope you do not mind."

"Certainly not. This has been a most delightful . . . surprise." She looked at me quickly but said nothing.

The schoolroom reminded me so much of Peter's and mine at Deerfield Hall that I felt a lump rise in my throat. The room was long with a low-beamed ceiling and many windows, each framed with bright-colored curtains. There were tables and chairs, and the walls were covered with colored maps and drawings and brightly painted cupboards. The whole effect was charming, truly a child's world. Judith grabbed my hand and led me around the room, exclaiming delightedly over globes, toys, games and maps.

"Just a moment, Andrea, I want you to see my Italian lessons," Judith commanded as she hurried to one of the cupboards.

Miss Gillbank came up to me, smiling. "I haven't the heart to scold her. It is such a pleasure to see her so excited with her schoolwork."

I turned to the governess and said with sincerity, "Judith is a very fortunate child to have you."

She disclaimed, "You are too kind, my lady!" Then she added thoughtfully, "You see, I love the child, and I have since the first time I saw her."

"How long have you been here at the manor, Miss Gillbank?"

"It has been nearly eight years now. It was my first position, and I do hope my last as well. I count myself very fortunate that Judith is such a loving, bright child."

Miss Gillbank was obviously a gentlewoman. I decided to speak frankly to her. "Judith was somewhat of a surprise to me. You see," I continued carefully, "I was not aware of her existence until she found me in the garden."

Miss Gillbank's brows rose, but she said only, "His lordship informed me last evening that Judith was to be presented to you this afternoon at tea. Perhaps," she added tentatively, "he wished to give you a pleasant surprise."

We looked at each other for a long moment in silence. I knew that she was as surprised and confused as I. What possible reason could Lawrence have for not telling me of his second wife . . . and Judith?

I remember something else that was bothering me. "Miss Gillbank, has Judith ever traveled to London or perhaps to Yorkshire? You see," I explained, "she looks familiar to me, and I thought perhaps I had seen her somewhere."

"No, Judith has never left Devbridge Manor . . . except of course, for occasional visits to Shropeshire, a small village to the west," she replied.

"Well, I suppose I must be mistaken," I said lightly, dismissing the topic.

We were examining Judith's Italian lessons and practicing some verb tenses when I happen to glance at the clock on the wall. "Oh, my dear," I exclaimed, "I did not realize the time!" I rose and shook out my skirts. Turning to Miss Gillbank, I added wryly. "I must go now and change for tea, or I will be late and in everyone's black books. Too, I do not wish to miss the lovely surprise Sir Lawrence planned for me!"

"No, no, of course we do not wish to be late either,"

said Miss Gillbank hurriedly. Judith clapped her hands together in anticipation.

"Oh, Miss Gillbank," I said, turning in the doorway. "We would be most pleased if you would dine with us this evening."

She looked momentarily surprised, but replied simply, "I would be delighted."

Could this be the first time she was to dine with the family? Surely not, I thought. If it was, her answer was all the proof I needed of her good breeding.

Later, in my room, I chose a gown of light yellow-crepe over a slip of white satin, with small puffed sleeves and fitted bodice. It was a summer gown, but the day was warm. Belinda arranged my hair charmingly. When I stepped back from my mirror, Belinda breathed in her soft country accent, "You're like a . . . a fairy, my lady, so light and delicate-looking."

Quite overcome, I responded, smiling, "Belinda, I do believe you're a flatterer."

"Oh, no, my lady, 'tis the truth," she exclaimed, shocked that I should think such a thing.

I turned back and looked into my mirror. A slender, elegant young woman stared back at me. I remembered then, during my first Season, several young gentlemen had nicknamed me the Fairy Princess. "What utter nonsense!" I had said scornfully. "Why I can seat a horse better than any of those . . . young puppies!"

Grandfather had roared with laughter. It seemed so long ago. A somewhat sad face stared at me now from the mirror. I shook my head at the sad image, thanked Belinda, and walked quickly from the room.

When I reached the drawing room, I stopped a moment to give my curls one final pat before entering. The door was slightly ajar, and I happened to hear Amelia say in a purring voice, "And what, my dear John, do you propose to call the chit—Mama . . . or perhaps Stepmama would be more appropriate."

My hands clenched into fists, and my jaw tightened. I was on the point of confronting Amelia when John replied, his voice deep and lazy, "Just so, Amelia. I believe for the moment that Andrea will suffice." His voice mocked.

Grandfather had always said that those who listen at doors will hear no good of themselves. He was right, but I found that I was almost rooted to the spot, unable either to leave or to enter.

John continued in his same lazy drawl, "You must admit, my dear, that we have been relieved of a great worry. At least the chit is not a scheming fortune hunter, as you so firmly believed!"

Amelia gave a high, metallic laugh. "Just so, John, but that leaves us with a rather interesting mystery, does it not?"

"What do you mean, sister?" John inquired.

"Why, I refer to the reason your father married the child."

"Or why she married my father," he added thoughtfully.

I was trembling. His shaft had hit too close to its mark for my peace of mind.

I heard Amelia's voice again, but could not make out her words.

John's response, however, was loud and clear. "Well, if he wishes to sire another brat, I applaud his endeavors!"

My face burned and my stomach felt as if I had been hit full strength with a fist. I grabbed up my skirts and ran blindly down the hall, John's deep laugh pursuing me.

I rushed into the Ladies' Parlour and slammed the door behind me with an angry bang. I pressed my hands against my flushed cheeks, but I was losing my battle against the rising tears. Suddenly I grabbed a Dresden figure from a table and flung it against the far wall. It shattered into tiny pieces across the floor. I stood staring at what I had done, feeling at once contrite but also less angry.

At that moment there was a knock at the door. In a voice that still shook, I called, "Yes, what is it?"

Brantley entered. His impassive countenance did not change at the sight of my flushed face and the shattered figure on the carpet. He paused slightly before saying in an even voice, "My lady, everyone awaits your presence in the drawing room."

"Yes, of course. Thank you, Brantley. I shall join them presently," I answered, rallying my forces.

In a voice devoid of expression he added, "I will inform his lordship that you will arrive . . . presently, my lady." It seemed to me that his face softened for a moment as he turned and closed the door quietly behind him.

I left the Ladies' Parlour a few moments later and made my way slowly back to the drawing room. Brantley was waiting for me at the door.

"Thank you, Brantley," I said as he opened the door for me.

I lifted my chin and walked firmly into the room.

FOUR

"There you are, my dear," said Lawrence. "Do come and sit down." He indicated a chair beside him. I murmured stiff hellos to Amelia, Thomas, and John and gave a special smile and greeting to Judith and Miss Gillbank.

"I understand you have met Judith and Miss Gillbank," Lawrence said at once.

"Yes," I answered, "a most charming and delightful . . . surprise."

"Just so, my dear," he acknowledged, avoiding my eyes.

Not wishing to draw attention to this topic, I quickly turned to Thomas and politely inquired after his day.

"Dashed like summer, that's what it is!" he exclaimed, mopping his brow with a fine lawn handkerchief.

"So fatiguing," Amelia agreed, waving a fine bone fan to and fro, but still managing to look deliciously cool in a pale pink silk gown.

Following a few more desultory comments on the

weather, Brantley entered, followed by a servant bearing cakes, macaroons, and tea. Amelia made an unconscious gesture toward the teapot, realized that it was now my office, and then leaned back again against the sofa, waving her fan with more energy than before. I kept my head down and commenced pouring the tea. Thomas, sensing his wife's discomfiture, filled the silence. "What do you think of Devbridge Manor, Andrea?"

"I have been most favorably impressed, especially with Sir Hugo," I replied. I turned to Lawrence and handed him his tea. "Sir Hugo certainly has the look of the devoted fanatic. You described him perfectly, sir."

"Our most unique ancestor." Lawrence smiled.

"I, too, find him most fascinating," said Miss Gillbank. "A stern taskmaster, undoubtedly."

"Oh, is he the one with the frightening little pig eyes?" asked Judith, her own eyes big as she fortified herself with another macaroon.

Thomas said, "That's him, Judith. How would you like him to take Clergyman Willcox' place?" He made a menacing gesture, and Judith shrieked in mock horror.

John said, "I've always felt it was a shame that Sir Hugo could not be our ghost. He would be a far more interesting specter."

My ears perked up. "Devbridge Manor has a ghost?"

"My dear, all great houses must have a resident ghost, just for appearances, you know," said Lawrence dryly.

Thomas added, "John is right, though. Our Blue Lady certainly does not have the flair of Sir Hugo."

"Who is the Blue Lady?" I asked.

"I believe the unfortunate young woman was a governess to my grandfather. Unluckily for her, the master of the house became . . . er . . . attracted to her and kept her in the north tower. To make the story brief," Lawrence said hurriedly, looking uneasily at Judith's rapt expression, "the wife discovered the liaison and did away with the poor governess."

"How did she do away with her, Father?" Judith asked excitedly.

"I believe she had her thrown from the top of the tower," Thomas answered, eyes gleaming.

"Oh, Miss Gillbank, isn't that horrible? You won't leave me now, Gilly, will you?" Judith cried.

Lawrence frowned at Thomas.

"I shall try to overcome my fears," Miss Gillbank said in an amused voice, and patted Judith's hand in reassurance.

"Have you ever seen the Blue Lady, sir?" Judith asked her father.

"I thought I did once," he admitted, "a long time ago. But it was probably too much stewed rabbit for dinner." Everyone laughed at this sally, and Judith looked relieved.

Conversation drifted into more general channels as teacups were refilled and macaroons and cakes were passed around again. Thomas very kindly engaged Miss Gillbank in conversation, and Lawrence inquired after Judith's educational pursuits. I noticed that Judith stood in some awe of her father, hanging on to his every word and trying to phrase her replies to his questions in a way that would please him.

A very pleasant half-hour passed in this way. Then Miss Gillbank said, "It is time for Judith's French lesson, so we must excuse ourselves." She rose gracefully and stretched out her hand to Judith. Judith looked mutinous for a moment. Miss Gillbank nodded smilingly to everyone and then turned to Lawrence. "With your permission, sir." He nodded, and turning to Judith, said, "My dear, I am depending upon you to be the accomplished linguist in the family." She smiled delightedly.

I rose with them and walked to the door. "May I come and visit you tomorrow, Judith?" I asked.

"Oh, yes, Andrea, you can help me finish my flour map of Greece," she offered.

"I should like that," I replied, remembering my own flour maps.

Miss Gillbank added, "You are most welcome at any time, my lady."

As they were walking out of the door past Brantley, I said, "Oh, Miss Gillbank, we will be expecting you for dinner this evening." My voice was loud enough for everyone to hear. If there were to be any disagreements, I wanted them now and not this evening in Miss Gillbank's presence.

She nodded and smiled. As soon as the door had closed behind them, Amelia said peevishly, "How considerate of you to invite Judith's governess to dine with the family. What other servants may we expect thrust upon us?"

Thomas, the peacemaker, hastily intervened. "Now, Amelia, my dear, Andrea means no harm. I am certain that—"

John interrupted his brother, saying, "Miss Gillbank is not a servant, Amelia, and if I am not mistaken in my facts, it is an unfortunate circumstance that is responsible for her being a governess."

"But she *is* a governess," Amelia snapped.

I said in an exasperated voice, "Besides being an intelligent and charming woman, Miss Gillbank is undoubtedly of gentle birth. On that I'll wager."

John turned to his father. "Is that true, Father? What is Miss Gillbank's background?"

Lawrence was looking rather contrite. He turned to me before responding to John. "You are perfectly right, my dear, and you also, John. Miss Gillbank comes from a very respectable family whose male heirs had an incurable penchant for the gaming tables. My sister, Lady Marcham, brought her to my attention . . . what was it? . . . seven or eight years ago. I invited her to Devbridge Manor, but I am certain that she would not have accepted the post had it not become known that her family had not a feather to fly with."

John was frowning in concentration. "Was not her father Carlton Gillbank?"

"Yes, that's right, John," Lawrence answered. "We heard later that he shot himself. A very sad business," he concluded, shaking his head.

Amelia sniffed audibly and gave Thomas what I would come to call That Look. He valiantly stepped into the breach. "But, Father, the fact does remain—"

Lawrence held up his hands to silence Thomas and, in fact, all of us, for I myself was preparing for battle. He said evenly, "No, Thomas, Amelia, the fact remains that we have been sadly remiss in our duty toward Miss Gillbank. As Andrea says, she is a charming, intelligent young woman of excellent breeding. And none of you will disagree that she has proven herself to be indispensable to Judith. It is time we showed her proper consideration."

Amelia shot me an angry look. Thomas merely looked uncomfortable. I felt sorry for Thomas, for he would have to be the one to endure any further tirades from Amelia on the subject.

John, on the other hand, had leaned back in his chair, dug his hands into his pockets, and had the look of one thoroughly amused. I gave him my most quelling frown, but it had no effect.

Amelia excused herself a few moments later and flounced from the room. Thomas accompanied her, a placating expression on his face.

As the door closed behind them, John said in his lazy

drawl, "Ah, such a passion for justice, and in one so young."

Trying to match his tone, I replied, "I had not realized that a passion for justice, as you phrase it, John, was limited to a certain age. Indeed," I continued coldly, "it appears that a passion for justice seems to be limited to only certain people also."

"Little cat," he said softly.

Before Lawrence could remonstrate with either of us, John abruptly turned to him and said, "I must be off, Father, to look at a hunter that Melham's put for sale." He rose, gave a careless bow in my direction, and walked briskly from the room.

Lawrence was frowning. "I apologize for my children. I had not realized that Amelia, in particular, was so terribly puffed up with her consequence. One would expect that sort of Gothic attitude from me, but certainly not from them," he concluded wryly.

Quite to my own surprise, I said, "But, Lawrence, John is also of your opinion and mine." What a strange creature you are, I said to myself. One minute you are arguing with John, and the next, you are defending him! Oh, well, fair was fair, and although John was rude and quite intolerable, he had not sided himself with Amelia and poor Thomas. Give the devil his due, I thought.

"True," Lawrence answered. "I am glad for that. Perhaps his travels have given him a more tolerant view of his fellowman. In any case, my dear, Miss Gillbank is quite delightful and I shall gladly welcome her."

"You are too kind, Lawrence. It is I who should beg your pardon, for I have sadly upset your household." I was beginning to feel contrite for the uncomfortable situation I had placed him in.

"Hush, my dear." He rose, sat down beside me, and patted my hand. There was silence between us for a few moments. Then he rose abruptly, took a turn about the room, and then returned to me. He began hesitantly, "I ah, am somewhat embarrassed, my dear. I suppose you have been wondering why I had not spoken to you of . . . Judith." His voice sounded strained and unnatural.

I had every intention of taking him to task for this omission, for it had caused me considerable embarrassment and unease. But seeing him so concerned and ashamed for his secrecy, I said only, "Yes, I was indeed surprised. But after all, Lawrence, it is of no great importance now. Judith is a sweet child and will be a great comfort to me."

I looked up at him hopefully, feeling quite proud of myself for taking such a magnanimous stance. But he was not content to let the subject be.

He stood up once again and began pacing. When he finally spoke, his voice was quite matter-of-fact, almost detached. "It was such a long time ago. Caroline was a lovely creature—so spirited and gay." A look of pain crossed his face, and he raised his hand as if to brush it away. I held my tongue, not knowing what to say, and waited for him to continue.

"It was only after I brought her back to Devbridge Manor that I began to understand her . . . true nature. It soon became apparent that she was ill." His voice was no longer matter-of-fact, it was filled with the pain of sad memories. I made to rise to go to him, but there was something in his face that made me stop. I said gently, "Lawrence, if you would prefer not to talk of it—"

He cut me off with an impatient wave of his hand. "No, it is only right that you understand about Judith." He continued after a brief moment. "At times Caroline would be gay and lively. But then suddenly her mood would change. She would neither speak nor eat. Thomas and John were scarce here in those days, but when they did come, she became worse. It seemed as though she resented their very existence. When she became pregnant, I hoped—and indeed the doctors predicted—that the child would cure her. But it did not. She became more withdrawn, more unpredictable. Toward the end, someone had to be with her at all times. We were afraid that she would try to harm herself . . . or the unborn child."

Ah, I thought to myself, the bars were for Caroline. Poor woman.

"But then, to everyone's surprise, when Judith was born, she seemed miraculously cured. You see, though, she was fooling all of us, and very cleverly, too." He was again silent, and I noticed that he was clenching and unclenching his hands in agitation. He turned his face away from me, and finally he whispered, "In her madness, she threw herself from the north tower. I shall never forgive myself for her death!"

I leaned toward him quickly and placed my hand on his arm. I was shaken over this sad and tragic story. "You mustn't blame yourself," I exclaimed. "It was an accident, Lawrence. She did not realize what she was doing. How could you have known?"

He turned back to me, his face pale and taut. "But, Andrea, I should have realized, should have guessed that it was a ruse. At least," he added grimly, "she did not kill the child."

I shuddered. We stayed as we were in silence for a moment before he exclaimed harshly, "Perhaps she should have carried Judith with her!"

"Why, for God's sake?" I exclaimed in horror.

"Do not you understand, Andrea? Judith is her seed. She left Judith to carry on her madness."

I recoiled. "Oh, no, Lawrence. Surely not. Why, Judith is a bright, normal child. I know it!"

"So was Caroline before she grew older," he responded grimly. Then he sighed. "Perhaps you may prove to be right. Miss Gillbank has worked wonders with the child. Before she came, we feared for Judith."

I frowned in disbelief, for Judith was only a toddler when Miss Gillbank arrived. Then Lawrence seemed to shake himself free of his painful memories. He looked at me and said in his normal, even voice, "That is why I was hesitant to tell you about Judith and, of course, about Caroline. Pure cowardice, my dear, pure cowardice. I hope that you will forgive me." He looked at me questioningly.

I felt a catch in my throat. "It is of no importance now." Then I added humbly, "Perhaps, Lawrence, if you will permit me, I can help you to forget."

A strange smile lit his face, and he said softly, "I am sure that you will, my dear. Very sure."

Dinner that evening was a gay affair. Amelia was in high spirits and seemed determined to please. When we had assembled in the drawing room, she nodded civilly to Miss Gillbank and complimented me on my blue silk gown. Perhaps Thomas was as adept at convincing as he was at making peace.

At the dinner table, Amelia was witty and altogether charming. John, seeming to fall in with her mood, became more animated and less withdrawn. When he recounted an anecdote about a certain Colonel Fitzpatrick, I found that he had a remarkable talent for mimicry. Amelia joined in the fun, and soon we were all laughing and trying to guess whom they were imitating.

The goodwill continued throughout the evening, to my profound relief. Miss Gillbank seemed to enjoy herself in her quiet, restrained way. She was certainly not out-of-place in such elevated company, I thought wryly. She would no doubt have been at ease and showed good sense were she in the presence of the regent himself.

When I finally got to bed that night, I snuggled under my warm covers contentedly and reviewed the happenings of the day in my mind. I thought of Miss Gillbank.

She was the kind of woman I would like to have for a friend. As I drifted into sleep, it occurred to me that I did not even know her first name. I would find out on the morrow, I decided.

I do not know why I awoke, for there was no sound, no whisper. But one moment I was peacefully sleeping and the next I was wide-awake, my eyes adjusting rapidly to the moonlit room.

There, standing motionless a few feet from my bed, was a figure. Cold fear gripped me. I felt my throat constrict with terror. My hand shot out toward the figure in a protective gesture as I pushed myself back violently, freeing myself from the heavy covers, until I was pressing against the back of my bed. The bell cord! Where was the bell cord? My hands searched frantically as my eyes stayed fixed on the figure.

The figure began to move slowly toward the bed. In that moment I could see the face clearly. It was an old woman, a hideous, wrinkled, misformed old woman. Wild, tangled white hair hung about her face. My mouth opened to scream, but only hoarse groaning sounds came out. In a cracked voice I heard myself cry, "Who are you? What do you want with me?"

To my unspeakable horror, the old woman whispered in a faraway voice, "You should not be here. Go, go, now!"

Sobbing with fear, I pulled myself to the far side of the bed, my eyes never leaving the horrible face. "Oh, my God, who are you, what do you want?" I gasped.

She did not answer but continued to move toward the bed. As she reached the dais, she lifted her arm. She was holding a knife, a long, slender blade, curved toward the tip. It was pointed in an arc above my breast!

I flung the cover away and hurled myself off the bed, stumbling over the night table. I flew to the door, knocking over a chair in my mad flight. As I wrenched the doorknob, I looked frantically back. The old woman had turned and was moving rapidly toward me, the knife blade still raised, gleaming horribly in the moonlight. The doorknob would not turn! I could hear myself crying pitifully and helplessly. Finally the knob turned under my frantic hands and I threw myself through the open doorway. I ran gasping in terror, down the long corridor.

My bare feet made no sound on the carpeted hall. I ran past the landing at the top of the stairway, gasping for breath. Then I saw a light beneath one of the doors. I ran to the door and pounded it with my fists, crying, "Please, please, let me in. Oh, God, someone help!" My voice broke into hoarse sobs and my knees gave way under me.

The door was thrown open in a violent gesture and John appeared. "What the devil!" he ejaculated.

I pulled myself up and threw myself against him, sobbing in relief. His arms went around me in a automatic, protective gesture. I clung to him, pressing close, my arms clutching his neck.

"Andrea, what is wrong—what has happened?" he cried, trying to ease my hold and shaking my shoulders.

I tried to speak, but the words seemed to crumble before I could utter them. John pulled me tightly against him again, stroking my hair. He said very gently, "It is all right now. You're safe, Andrea." His voice was soothing, as if he were quieting a frightened animal.

The terror began slowly to recede. I felt his chest next to my cheek, damp with my tears. I looked up, and felt my hair brushing against his face. His eyes were deep, fathomless in the dim light. He still held me tightly against him with one arm. He brought his other hand to my face and brushed away damp tendrils of hair from my forehead. He rested his hand lightly against my cheek. I closed my eyes for a moment, trying to control my unsteady breathing. He cupped my chin in his hand and gently pushed my face up. I opened my eyes and met his gaze. His eyes were narrowed and he looked stern, but his voice was gentle as he again inquired, "Come, now, try to tell me what has happened."

I took a deep breath but did not draw away from him. I felt as though I would lose my courage without him. I began haltingly, "There was a woman . . . an old woman. Oh, God, it was horrible!" I gasped, unable to speak for a moment. I then looked up into John's face and whispered, "She t-tried to kill me!"

"Someone tried to kill you?" he repeated in shocked surprise. "How can this be possible?" he exclaimed.

At that moment Lawrence came hurrying down the hall. "John, Andrea, what is wrong, what has happened?" he cried.

"Father . . . quickly, take her," John ordered, as he pulled my arms away from him and pushed me toward Lawrence. He ran quickly toward the west wing.

Lawrence gently shook my shoulders, and repeated urgently, "My dear, what is it?"

Before I could answer, Amelia and Thomas appeared. "Good heavens, Father, what is all this commotion?" Amelia demanded sharply.

Lawrence replied uncertainly, "Andrea has suffered some sort of fright." Then he turned to me. "My dear, you must be chilly. Come, you must sit down." His voice was calm and matter-of-fact. I allowed myself to be led to a small parlour down the hall. Lawrence sat beside me on the sofa, gently rubbing my hands.

"Here, Father, here is a dressing gown," Thomas offered.

I clutched the heavy material against me, and felt warmth return.

"Now," Lawrence said, "tell us what has upset you so, my dear."

I looked up at the three faces staring at me expectantly. I took a deep breath and began. "There was an old woman, a horribly ugly old woman, in my room." Disbelieving eyes stared at me, but I continued, more calmly now, "She was standing near my bed." I stopped a moment and ran my hand distractedly through my hair. I gritted my teeth and said what I knew sounded fantastic. "She had a knife . . . and she tried to kill me. I . . . I ran."

Lawrence was looking at me intently, his lips pursed and his brows drawn together. Thomas was gaping at me in utter disbelief. Amelia said acidly, "What a lively imagination you have, Andrea! One would wish, however," she added with a deprecating gesture, "that you would stage your dramatics at a more convenient hour!"

Thomas intervened quickly. "Undoubtedly a bad dream. Yes, that's what it was, a bad dream," he repeated.

"Oh, no," I cried, "I saw her. She did try to kill me!" My eyes flew to my husband's face, pleading.

Lawrence leaned over and took my hand in his. "In any event, my dear, you have suffered a great shock." After a brief pause he added, "Of course, we will look into this matter."

"Really, Father . . ." Amelia began.

Before she could continue, John hastened into the room and strode over to me. He said evenly, "I have searched your room . . . and all the other bedrooms. I found no one. Of course," he continued quickly, looking at my drawn face, "there was certainly sufficient time for the old woman to escape."

I looked away quickly, pressing my hand against my mouth to keep from crying out.

"There, you see," Amelia said triumphantly. "It is all her imagination!"

Indignation at Amelia's words washed over me. I

willed myself to look at all of their faces, staring at me. Gritting my teeth, I repeated, "The old woman was real and she tried to kill me." I looked at each of them in turn. "I cannot believe that you disbelieve me. Do you think me a hysterical child?" I demanded.

John made a movement toward me but stopped when his father said quickly, "My dear, certainly you thought you saw something, or someone. But consider," he continued reasonably, "you are in a strange house. And there was all our talk about the Blue Lady this afternoon. Do you not think, my child, that this would be sufficient to make anyone see things?"

"Your logic is impeccable," I said bitterly. "But, Lawrence, I know what I saw. It did happen!" I looked up at John. He was frowning, his mouth set into grim lines. I supposed he did not believe me either. I was beginning to feel numb.

Amelia yawned elaborately and said, "Well, I for one am going back to bed." She sniffed, turned on her heel, and marched from the room. Thomas looked uncertain, and finally followed his wife.

"Come, my dear," Lawrence said gently, "I will take you back to your room." I stiffened perceptibly. He hastened to add, "Andrea, I will have the house and grounds, thoroughly searched tomorrow morning. If there was an intruder, we will find her."

I did not immediately take his proffered arm, but gazed up into his face. "I am not a silly child, Lawrence, to be scared by bogeys. What I have told you is true." With what dignity I could muster, I rose and clutched the dressing gown around me. I did not look again at John as I walked slowly past him through the door.

My courage deserted me when we reached the Blue Room. I drew back, unwilling to enter. Lawrence said calmly, "Do not worry. I will search in here. Then you can lock the door. There is no other entrance." I nodded mutely and remained in the doorway until Lawrence returned, saying, "All is well. There is no one here."

When he left, I locked the door quickly and ran to my bed. I burrowed under the covers, trembling. I could not prevent my eyes from going to the place where the old woman had stood.

Sleep eluded me until near dawn. Every time I began to drift off, my eyes would fly open and probe every corner of the room. Near dawn, I fell into a fitful sleep and did not awake until the morning was well advanced.

When I finally awoke, sunlight filled the room. My eyes flew again instantly to the spot where the old woman had stood.

In the cheerful morning light, even I doubted myself for a brief moment. "No," I said aloud, "I did not imagine anything. The old woman will be found."

I dressed quicky, without ringing for Belinda. I wanted to get downstairs as quickly as possible to find my husband. I was certain that he would have found the old woman. I shivered, thinking of the raised knife, of her horrible face. It had been the first time in my life I had known terror, the terror of the unknown and the terror of dying. But, again, as I looked around the cheerful, sunlit Blue Room, I wondered how such a thing could be possible.

As I crossed the Old Hall toward the morning room, I met Brantley.

"Good morning, my lady," he said smoothly. I glanced up at him sharply, wondering how much he knew of last night's disturbance. His countenance was impassive, as usual.

"Good morning, Brantley," I responded. "Have you seen his lordship this morning?"

He bowed slightly and said, "I will inform his lordship, my lady."

"Thank you, Brantley. I shall be in the morning room," I said.

Ella served my breakfast. Her face was alight with curiosity, unlike Brantley's. Anger rose in me, for obviously the servants were aware of only one telling of the story. I dismissed her as quickly as possible. I had nearly finished my breakfast when Lawrence entered. I stood quickly, my hands gripping the sides of the table. He crossed to me quickly and brushed his lips lightly against my cheek.

"Lawrence?" My voice was sharp.

I knew his answer before he spoke. He shook his head and said soothingly, "I am sorry, Andrea. I had the entire house and grounds searched thoroughly. There was no evidence of an intruder."

"I see," I responded stiffly. I had been so sure that someone or something would be found. This was fantastic! What if someone in the house did not wish the old woman to be found? I asked myself. What if someone wanted me to doubt my senses or convince everyone else that I was unbalanced? I was on the edge of saying something of the sort to my husband when I realized that he was treating me with all of the troubled concern one would accord to an overwrought, hysterical woman. Good God, did he think me another Caroline? Getting a grip on myself, I said calmly, trying to smile, "Doubtless you were correct, Lawrence, in your analysis last night," I amended. "A strange place—and the stewed rabbit, of course."

Lawrence looked relieved, and I felt that I had chosen the right course of action. He said, smiling, "Do not forget also our incumbent ghost, the Blue Lady."

"A very frightening combination, to be sure," I commented lightly. "Would you like a cup of coffee, Lawrence?" I asked, reaching for the pot. What a normal, domestic scene, I thought, as we sat drinking our coffee.

No one would ever imagine our topic of conversation!

After a few minutes Lawrence said in a mysterious voice, "When you have finished your breakfast, Andrea, I have a surprise awaiting you outside."

I looked at him questioningly, but he would say no more. Anxious to prove to him that I had now returned to being a rational person, I said, smiling, "A surprise! Oh, do let us go at once!"

He seemed pleased at my excited response, for he rose immediately. A ubiquitous footman opened the great front door for us to pass out. There, at the foot of the steps, stood a groom holding the reins of a magnificent bay stallion. He was pulling up and down against the groom's hand, his unclipped mane flying. A full sixteen hands high he was, with graceful sloping shoulders, a long back, and a triangle patch of white that stood out on his forehead. He looked both strong and spirited.

I was truly excited and gasped in delight. "Oh, Lawrence, is he for me?" Before he could respond, I was skipping quickly down the front steps.

"His name is Dante, Andrea. I hope that you like him," Lawrence called after me.

"Like him!" I exclaimed. "Of a certainty I shall!"

I slowed as I reached the bottom step, not wishing to frighten him. As I came closer, Dante began to dance nervously from side to side. The groom was having difficulty holding him.

"It's frisky he is this morning, my lord," the groom called to Lawrence.

"Oh, dear, I haven't any sugar. That would surely calm him."

"Here ye are, milady," said the groom, handing me some sugar from his jacket pocket.

"Pull down firmly on his bridle," I said, as I advanced quietly toward Dante, sugar on my outstretched, flattened palm. The groom did as I bid, and Dante calmed.

He looked at me suspiciously, jerking his head slightly. But evidently his greed overcame his suspicions, for he began nuzzling my hand and nibbling up the sugar cubes. When he finished, my hand was thoroughly wet but free of sugar. He snorted, looking at me expectantly. I shook my head at him and said, grinning, "Oh, no you don't, Dante. It is time you did something for me. I promise, more sugar for you later!"

I held out my hand toward the groom for the reins. The groom looked uncertainly at Lawrence for instructions. My husband nodded. As I took the reins, Dante again began prancing from side to side. I held the bridle firmly in one hand and began to stroke his soft forehead with the other. I spoke to him as Grandfather had taught me. I whispered his name and countless endearments. I thought to myself: If he does not stop soon, my arm will be too tired to control him. I said softly to him, "Come, Dante, quiet down and I shall give you all the sugar you can manage." After a moment he neighed, tossed his head in seeming satisfaction at my proposal, and quieted.

"More sugar," I demanded, holding my hand out to the groom. "I always keep my promises." I offered him the rest of the sugar, and when he had finished, he playfully nudged his head against my shoulder. I laughed with pleasure and hugged his big head against me. I heard the groom say to Lawrence, "Her ladyship's got a right proper light hand, milor'."

"Indeed she does," Lawrence affirmed proudly.

I turned. "May I ride him now, Lawrence? It will take me but a moment to change."

"Certainly, my dear." He turned toward the groom. "William has been training him to sidesaddle. You should have no difficulty with him."

I relinquished the reins, saying, "I shall be back in ten minutes, William. Continue walking him around, if you please."

I squeezed Lawrence's arm as I passed him. "Thank you, sir. You are too good, too kind."

"Be gone with you, child," he returned, laughing.

I raced up the stairs and down the corridor to my room. I rang for Belinda and began struggling out of my clothes. Belinda appeared and regarded me wide-eyed.

"Quickly, Belinda, my blue velvet riding habit—also my hat and boots!"

In a remarkably short time my plumed hat was fastened securely over my hair and I was hurrying back downstairs. As I ran down the wide staircase, I held up my skirts, intent on watching my feet so that I would not stumble. When I reached the foot of the stairs, I let my skirts fall and looked up. John was standing directly in front of me, an amused look on his face. He was also clad in riding clothes. Suddenly I felt very shy.

"G-good morning, John," I stammered, my eyes avoiding his.

"Good morning," he returned in his lazy drawl. "I trust you were not disturbed the remainder of the night." I looked up at him quickly. His searching look belied the indifference of his voice.

Recalling the scene, I felt painfully embarrassed. I felt a flush creep over my face. I remembered how I had thrown myself against him, clad only in my thin nightgown, my hair loose about my shoulders. His hands had stroked my hair and I had pressed my face against his bare chest. I remembered all too clearly the warmth and strength of his body against mine, his powerful arms holding me tight. With my embarrassment I also felt shame, shame at the strange and unwanted feelings that now passed through me as I recalled the scene. I tried to cover my confusion but succeeded only in drawing attention to my obvious discomfort. I tried to explain.

"I am most truly . . . sorry for bursting in on you

. . . in such an unseemly manner. It was just that . . . what I mean is—"

He interrupted me with a wave of his hand. "Do not refine upon it, Andrea. 'Tis forgotten," he said quietly. Then he said abruptly, "I see that you are dressed for riding." He had saved me from further embarrassment, and I was grateful. I felt the flush recede from my cheeks. I said quickly, "Yes, I am riding. Your father has given me a beautiful bay stallion. Do come, John, and see him."

A footman threw open the door for me as I hurried past John.

"Look, John," I cried pointing at Dante, "is he not beautiful?"

John did not answer. Instead, he strode down the steps two at a time and confronted his father. "Father, you cannot seriously think of allowing Andrea to ride Dante. You know very well he is not fit for a lady, much less one of her size!" He indicated my small figure with a disdainful wave.

I had followed him quickly down the steps and now wheeled on him, "How dare you, John—" I began.

John interrupted abruptly. "Don't be a fool, you know very well that you could not possibly handle that horse! Good God, just look at the size of him!"

"You have no right, do you hear, John, no right whatsoever to dictate—"

"Now, both of you listen a moment," Lawrence said with calm authority. He turned to John. "I assure you, my dear boy, that Andrea is an excellent horsewoman. I would not insult her by giving her one of the ladies' hacks."

I raised my chin and looked triumphantly at John.

"But, sir—" he began.

"No, John. You will trust my judgment and good sense in this matter. Could you ever seriously doubt, even for a moment, that I would take any chances with her safety?"

Before John could respond, I added coldly, "John, your concern is hardly necessary."

Lawrence turned to me quickly and gave me a look that made me feel like a spoiled, naughty child. It made me want to sink for my want of decent manners.

"Now, that is enough—from both of you!" he said firmly. "Let us enact no more scenes."

I flushed at the reprimand. The groom, William, was gazing at us, a wide grin on his face.

"I'm . . . sorry," I muttered stiffly, my eyes down. John said nothing, but I could feel his anger.

Lawrence said suddenly, "I have an excellent idea. John, you shall accompany Andrea. Then you can judge her skill for yourself!"

I wanted to protest, but thought better of it and remained silent. John, too, seemed hesitant, but finally said in a growl, "Very well, sir."

Then he said coldly to me, "You will wait here. I will return in a few minutes." He walked quickly away toward the stables.

How dare he give me orders, I raged silently. As if reading my thoughts, Lawrence said, chuckling, "Do not mind him, my dear. I think his years of campaigning have made him a bit . . . autocratic."

"Humph," I said.

Lawrence then took my chin in his hand and said, "Don't be so upset, my dear. After all, John is an expert horseman and his concern is only for your safety."

I realized that I was beginning to appear ridiculous, and scolded myself. I said, "You are perfectly right, sir. I will contrive to conduct myself in a less hurly-burly manner."

Lawrence gave a shout of laughter. "Please, please,

spare me that! Believe me, Andrea, a paragon of ladylike virtue would be an intolerable bore."

My lips twitched. "Well, at least," I conceded, "I shall contrive to be less vocal in front of the servants."

"A handsome concession, to be sure," Lawrence replied, looking at the grinning William. "But even our servants are well used to the unpredictable ways of the Devbridges!"

At that moment Dante neighed and reached his head toward me. "Just a moment, my beautiful one," I cooed.

I suddenly thought to ask, "Oh, Lawrence, why is he named Dante?"

"I am glad you asked, for I was quite meaning to tell you that story. You see, I bought him, strangely enough, from a French count, who had an incurable passion for the Italian classics. He felt if the horse were named Dante, he would know all the places to avoid."

I giggled. "You mean, Lawrence, that the horse was to whinny nine times when the count went to Paris?"

"Something like that, I would imagine. But I am not sure if Paris is quite as bad as the ninth circle of hell!" he returned, grinning.

At that moment John cantered toward us on a huge black stallion. His long sloping shoulders rippled with strength and suppressed energy. Like his master, I thought.

"Whenever your ladyship is ready," John said coolly, putting needless emphasis on "ladyship," I thought angrily.

I shot him a haughty look, turned my back on him, and allowed myself to be tossed up into the saddle by the groom. When I had settled myself comfortably and the groom had adjusted the stirrup, I signaled for the bridle to be released. Dante stood still for one moment. Then, as I tugged lightly on the reins, he gave a snort and reared on his hind legs. As Lawrence and the groom hurried forward, I held up my hand and cried laughingly, "Oh, no, he is but being playful. I assure you, Lawrence, he is well under control!"

"Are you very sure, my dear?" Lawrence asked, his brow creased.

"Please, Lawrence, trust me," I said as softly as I could, not wishing John to overhear. John, in the meanwhile, sat his horse quietly, scowling at the scene.

I tightened my grip slightly. Dante tossed his mane and began to sidle in little prancing steps. But when he realized that I was indeed there to stay, he neighed, looked back at me, and became quiet.

"You see, we shall deal famously together." Although I directed my words to my husband, they were meant for John. I gazed quickly at him, my chin high. He looked quite unconvinced but forbore to comment.

"Are you ready?" I asked coolly.

"Certainly, ma'am—when you have your horse under control," came the provoking response.

"I assure you I am quite settled now, sir," I snapped.

John wheeled his horse around beside Dante. I loosed my grip, and we cantered sedately down the long drive.

"Have an enjoyable ride," Lawrence called. I turned and waved my hand in response.

The graveled front drive melted into the wooded park that surrounded the east side of Devbridge Manor. The path, as it was called, was large enough to accommodate a chaise, so we remained side by side.

The warm sunlight filtered through the brilliantly colored leaves. Autumn was coming, but slowly. I sighed in sheer contentment. As we emerged from the wooded park, I pulled up and turned to John. "I would like to shake out the fidgets. What is the best spot for a long gallop?"

"I do not think it wise for you . . ." he began.

I threw him an impatient glance, dug my heels, and

wheeled Dante to the lane that branched to the right. He reared slightly, and then, sensing imminent freedom, put his head down and broke into a gallop. I heard John yell after me angrily, "Go ahead—break your damned neck!"

I turned and waved to him gaily. "Come, faintheart," I shouted mockingly. Within a few moments he was riding at my side, his face set in grim lines.

I threw back my head, feeling the wind whip my hair loose from my riding hat. I gave a shout of joy and urged Dante to a faster pace. He was surefooted, his stride long and steady.

I felt that I was back in the hills of Yorkshire, galloping wildly and freely against the wind. I leaned forward and stroked Dante's neck, feeling his muscles ripple under my gloved hand. "You're magnificent, my beautiful Dante," I crooned.

I heard John shout something at me. I jerked up and saw a phaeton coming around a sharp bend ahead of us, racing toward us, drawn by two steaming horses. I looked around quickly. The phaeton could never slow in time, and there was not enough room for our horses to pass beside it. We must pull up at the very edge of the lane and allow the phaeton to pass. In a moment, John was beside me, his muscles taut, hand poised to grab my reins. I jerked sharply on Dante's bridle, wheeling him out of reach of John's outstretched hand. I heard him curse.

"Devil's to pay," I shouted over my shoulder, "but I will not want your help!"

From the corner of my eye I saw that John had slowed and was on the opposite side of the lane. In a swift movement I pulled back with all my strength on the reins. Nothing happened! Dante jerked his head down, nearly tearing the reins from my hands, and galloped faster, straight for the oncoming phaeton.

I threw myself against his neck, as high as I could

reach. I grasped each rein as closely to his mouth as possible, and wrapping the reins tightly around my fists, I abruptly jerked the reins down and then back. He snorted in sudden pain and surprise and tried to pull free of the strong pressure on his mouth. I held fast and jerked down again, harder. He slowed to a canter, and as the pressure did not lessen, finally to a walk. I pressed him quickly to the very edge of the ditch at the side of the lane. The phaeton whirled past us in a cloud of dust as both Dante and I remained motionless and panting with exertion. Not one moment too soon, I thought grimly. I looked down. The ditch beside the lane was deep, and a double fence prevented jumping. I heaved a deep breath. I felt a bit shaky, but resolved not to let John know.

I looked up, to see John crossing over to me.

"Well, John, are you now convinced that I won't break my damned neck?" I was thankful that he could not see my shaking hands.

"Where did you learn that trick?" he exploded.

"Why, from my grandfather—when I was twelve years old," I responded lightly, my chin going up. I added to myself: If you hadn't been able to do that, my girl, you might very well be lying on the ground with a broken neck!

But I did not say that to John. Rather: "Come, won't you admit that I can handle Dante without your assistance?"

"You were lucky this time," he said harshly.

"How ungenerous of you," I said lightly, leaning over and patting Dante's steaming neck.

He was silent for a moment, his eyes narrowed. Then he grinned. "Touché, madam. My humble apologies for my unnecessary interference!"

I jerked up, giving him a look of sheer astonishment. He laughed. "Are you so surprised that I can admit to a mistake in judgment? I assure you, ma'am, that I am not so inflexible or intolerant!"

As I continued to stare at him, without a word to say, he added wryly, "Father was right—you're an excellent horsewoman!"

I struggled with myself for a moment before my better self won. "That is exceedingly kind of you to say, John. But you saw, I am certain, that I did indeed have some . . . difficulty. But, of course, I managed very well," I finished defiantly.

"Did I not just this moment fully admit to that fact?" he inquired sweetly.

"Yes, of course, but—"

"Then why do you continue to apologize?" he mocked.

I glared at him in silence, unable to put two words together. Then my sense of humour overcame my shattered pride and I began to giggle and then to laugh in earnest. John looked at me, grinning. As I wiped my streaming eyes, I exclaimed, "You are a devil, Master Jack, and quite odious and abominable to boot!"

"Really, ma'am, I must protest—"

"Oh, no, you don't." It was my turn to interrupt "You already put me into full retreat, and I thought that I had won the battle! No more skirmishes, sir, until I have rallied my forces!"

"Madam, my lips are sealed!" He doffed his hat and proffered a deep bow.

"John, do be careful, you will fall!" I cried as his bow nearly unseated him.

He straightened, his eyes twinkling wickedly. "Cry peace?" he asked.

"Cry peace," I agreed, suddenly shy. Our eyes held for a moment.

Abruptly he wheeled his horse away from me. "You will notice the cottages across the field," he called to me, pointing to the north.

My eyes followed his pointing finger. "Yes. Are they our people?" I asked.

"Yes, the majority of our tenant farmers live in this area. Beyond the hills is more grazing land."

"I should like to meet them," I said.

"As lady of the manor, you of course will," he responded. "If my lamentable memory serves me right, it is a Devbridge tradition for the servants and all the tenants to attend a special Christmas ball. You will give out gifts to the children, and Father will distribute a few guineas to the parents." He had lapsed back into his familiar drawl. He was obviously bored.

I persevered and replied, "It is a very common tradition, I believe. We had something of the sort yearly at Deerfield Hall, in Yorkshire." Receiving no response to this information, and seeing no future for this conversation, I turned in the saddle and pointed to the heavily wooded area to our left. "What is in that direction?" I inquired.

"It is a continuation of the home woods. There are many paths running through the wood to the lake."

This was interesting. "I would like very much to see the lake, that is, if you do not mind," I added.

"Not at all," he responded politely. "The paths are narrow, so you will have to follow after me. And slowly, if you do not mind," he added blandly.

"In this circumstance, I think it quite unexceptionable," I said meekly.

He gave me a twisted grin, click-clicked to his horse, and continued up the lane at a sedate pace. He stopped at several points along the lane to check for a path leading through the woods. After one such examination he turned back to me and said, "Here we are. The path's a bit grown over, but I think it's clear enough for us to get through."

"Lead on," I called.

I turned off after him into the woods. The path was overgrown and the horses had difficulty picking their way for several yards. The trees were so thick that sunlight came through the branches as long shafts of light. I had to put my arm up to push overhanging branches out of the way.

"Master Jack, is it much farther? I fear I will loose my riding hat any minute to an elm tree."

"We're almost there," he said, turning in his saddle.

In a few moments we came through the trees into a large open meadow with tall waving grass and a few hardy wildflowers. I drew in my breath in delight, for the meadow sloped gently to the lake. It was a lovely prospect. The lake was narrow, but obviously long, curving in either direction out of my view. The water was placid and a clear blue-green.

"How lovely it is!" I exclaimed. Does the lake extend as far back as the manor, John?" I asked as I slid from Dante's back.

"Yes," he responded, "it is about three miles long, but not at all wide, as you can see."

John also dismounted and took Dante's reins from my hand and led both horses to a sturdy-looking bush nearby to tether them.

"They're going to make great pigs of themselves," I observed, watching Dante and John's stallion, Drago, begin to feast on the waving blades of grass.

"True," he responded promptly, "but Dante in particular is most deserving of nourishment after his trying morning!"

I was instantly goaded, but I stopped myself. "No, John, I shan't cross swords with you right now." With that I sank down onto the soft grass at the edge of the water and gave him the most docile expression I could muster.

He sat down beside me and said, grinning, "All right, Madam Innocence, what are you about now?"

I looked primly down at my gloved hands and began idly twiddling my thumbs.

"I have the most awful feeling that I am going to be most foully murdered at any moment," he observed with mock horror in his voice.

"Oh, no, John," I replied quickly, "'tis only that I want to know something, and it appears that you are willing to be a 'comfortable' companion only when I am a docile, bending female."

One black brow shot up. "I pity the man who has the schooling of you," he said with strong conviction.

"You forget, John, I am already married," I said quietly.

There was a long moment of silence. Then he replied, "Yes, I was forgetting. Rest assured that it will not happen again."

There was another pause, and then he continued, lapsing again into his indifferent, bored voice, "And what is it that you wished to know, ma'am? I am, of course, at your service."

I covered my rising indignation and hurt by saying quickly, "Please tell me about Peter—my brother."

He did not answer immediately but rather picked up a pebble at his elbow and flung it carelessly into the lake and watched it take several skips before sinking. He turned to me and said, "There's not much to tell. We campaigned together on the Peninsula, and, of course, at Waterloo. He is a brave man," he added.

"Not that," I said quickly. "I mean your exploits, you know, adventures, what it was like in Spain and Belgium."

"Do not refine too much on army life. I assure you," he said flatly, "there was but a lot of mud, fleas and . . . whores."

He succeeded in shocking me, for my eyes grew wide. Even Grandfather at his spiciest had never been so explicit or so crude.

To avoid looking at him, I leaned forward and rippled my fingers through the water. It seemed as though he were purposely trying to hurt me.

"I apologize, Andrea," he said gently after a brief moment. He sounded sincere. I looked up at him quickly.

He gave a wry smile and said with effort, "You see, I do not wish to speak about . . . that life, at the moment. It was not romantic—simply foul, dirty, and there was . . . the butchery of Waterloo . . ." His voice trailed off.

Without thinking, I reached out my hand and laid it on his arm. It was I who had hurt him by prying into painful memories. I said softly, "I am sorry, John, I did not realize . . ."

The grimness on his face vanished and he put his hand over mine.

I said tentatively, "Peter was loath to speak about his campaigns, particularly Waterloo."

He gave his head a slight shake, as if he were warding off the blackness of his memories.

"Give me a while longer, Andrea. Then we will speak of Peter's and my exploits."

Then he turned from me and gazed out over the lake. There was need for a new topic of conversation, for our silence was not a comfortable one.

"Are there rowboats?" I asked.

"Yes. The boathouse is around the bend, toward the manor. If you wish," he added, "we will check the boats to see if they're still seaworthy."

"I should like that very much," I pursued, thinking that this, at least, was an unexceptionable topic. "When may we check the boats?"

"Whenever you please," he replied indifferently.

I could think of nothing more to say for the moment, so I simply settled back, removed my riding hat, and discovered to my chagrin that my hair was hanging loose about my shoulders.

"Oh, my, it appears I have come quite undone," I remarked ruefully, more to myself than to John. As I straightened my hair, John turned back to me and said in a serious, meditative tone, "I want you to tell me about last night. Tell me everything that happened."

I dropped a heavy plait of hair that I was in the process of pinning back into place. To me, this was certainly not a comfortable topic, and I wished, for the moment, to forget about it. I frowned, pursed my lips, and continued working assiduously with my hair. But John was not one to take a hint.

"Come, Andrea," he said impatiently, "you would not now pretend that you imagined or dreamed your nocturnal visitor, would you?"

I raised my chin and spoke in what I hoped was a voice of dismissal. "I would prefer not to speak of it just now, John, just as you do not wish to speak of your campaigns."

"But there is a big difference, ma'am. I am part of your adventure. You had nothing whatsoever to do with mine."

I opened my mouth to protest, but was interrupted. "The old woman, or ghost, or whatever the devil it was, is very much my affair. You tumbled me into it, if you will remember."

I bit my lower lip, glared at him, and then acquiesced. "Very well, if you must," I replied, hunching a shoulder. I was silent for another moment, gathering my thoughts, forcing myself to relive the previous night.

I began slowly, diffidently. "Are you not aware, John, that no one . . . nothing was found this morning?"

"Of course," he returned shortly. "I was very much a

part of the hunt." He waved his hand indifferently, as if to dismiss it. "That was this morning. I did not expect to find anything, and if you did"— he paused and looked at me searchingly—"you were deluding yourself. Whoever or whatever it was would certainly not stay about to be trapped. Now, tell me again what happened. Leave nothing out," he commanded.

Thus adjured, I began to recount and relive the old woman, the knife, and ended with my wild flight to his door. As I spoke, I felt gooseflesh rise on my arms. When I had finished my recital, John's eyes narrowed in concentration, and he rapped out, "Is that everything? Are you sure you have left out nothing?"

I nodded, silent. But then I did remember something else. "No, wait. The old woman spoke," I cried, pressing my fingers against my temples, trying to remember.

"Well, what did she say?" he asked impatiently.

My brow furrowed in concentration. Slowly the words came back to me.

"She said something like, 'You do not belong here, you should go.' Oh, I am not sure now, John," I cried, shaking my head.

To my surprise, John said nothing, and his face did not give me a clue to his thoughts. He was absently pulling up blades of grass and chewing on them.

"You know, John," I continued after a moment, "it was as if she did not really wish to harm me . . . perhaps just to frighten me."

There was no reply.

Finally John straightened and turned to me abruptly, saying, "There is a marked resemblance between you and Peter."

I looked at him questioningly, wondering why this would occur to him at such a moment.

He continued. "It is not just the physical likeness,

though it is marked." He shook his head. "No, it is more the similarity of your temperaments."

"You refer to our marked penchant for stubbornness?" I asked, smiling.

"That, of course," he returned quickly. "It is more. You know that Peter has a strong streak of common sense."

"Yes," I replied, "Peter's feet are firmly planted on solid ground." Yes, I thought to myself, Peter was always so sure of himself and of what he wanted. Could I say the same for myself?

John interrupted my wandering thoughts. "This is precisely what I mean. You see, Peter would never imagine or dream a ghostly apparition. It is simply not in his nature to do so." He stood up abruptly and brushed off his breeches. "As I said, there is a great likeness between the two of you."

Before I could respond, he held out his hand to help me rise. "It is time to go back. My father will be wondering if either Dante or I have broken your neck." His voice and manner were flippant. It seemed as though our serious conversation had never occurred.

I allowed him to help me to my feet. We walked in silence to our horses. He tossed me lightly in the saddle, and we returned back through the woods to the lane and then back to the manor.

When we reached the front steps, I prepared to dismount, when John commanded me peremptorily to wait. I looked at him, frowning, much disliking his orders. He dismounted and walked to me and held up his hands to lift me down.

"You must think of your consequence," he commented dryly. "Whatever would the servants say, particularly our staid Brantley, if they witnessed the Countess of Devbridge jumping off her horse unassisted?"

My frown became an instant smile. "Certainly a grave consideration," I affirmed, eyes twinkling.

John lifted me down. He then turned and led both horses to the stables.

I stood quietly for a moment, gazing after him, perplexed at all that had happened during the morning. I found John baffling. At one moment he treated me with indifferent boredom and the next moment with a calm assumption of authority that I found insufferable. But then, I thought, there was his kindness of the previous night and his obvious concern while we sat by the lake. Thus occupied in unraveling confused thoughts, I entered the manor and crossed to the staircase.

"My lady," came Brantley's voice behind me.

I turned. "Yes, Brantley?"

"Lord and Lady Applecroft and Miss Applecroft are in the drawing room."

I raised my brows in a question, for these names were unknown to me.

Brantley explained. "Lord and Lady Applecroft are our nearest neighbors, their establishment being situated about a mile from the manor." His tone implied that the Applecrofts were worthy of due consideration, but not, of course, of the same quality as the Earl of Devbridge.

I smiled and nodded in understanding. "Is his lordship with them?"

"Yes, my lady, as are Lady Amelia and Master Thomas."

"Very well, please inform our guests and his lordship that I am but just now returned from riding and will be with them presently."

I hurried up the stairs for the second time this day, stripping off my gloves as I went.

Belinda had already laid out a suitable morning gown.

"Why, thank you, Belinda," I said, pleased. I presumed

that the light blue muslin was the appropriate apparel for the likes of the Applecrofts.

She blushed and bobbed a curtsy. "I didn't want your ladyship to be fidgetin' around when there were visitors," she explained as she unfastened buttons, arranged pleats, and twitched folds. I marveled at her quick efficiency. A scant twenty minutes later, I was entering the drawing room.

Lady Applecroft dominated the company. She was a large woman of indeterminate years, dressed in a striking purple full-skirted gown and an equally striking turban set firmly over tightly crimped curls. She was wearing a wide smile when I entered, showing too many large teeth. Lord Applecroft, unlike his spouse, was slight of build and affected the height of fashion. His shirt points were starched so stiffly that he could scarce move his head, and his cravat was tied in a marvelous creation. His apparel was completed by an elegant waistcoat in bright green and breeches of pale yellow. He was a grand sight, to be sure. He was gazing at me in frank admiration, and I caught the knowing look in his eyes. Peter would undoubtedly have termed him a loose fish at first glance.

Lady Applecroft's smile grew wider as she said, "Come, Lucinda, and make your curtsy to her ladyship." Lucinda was a pretty girl, not at all like her mother or father, and newly emerged from the schoolroom. I supposed that she was probably anticipating her first Season in the spring. She was fair-complexioned with large cornflower-blue eyes and a small pouting mouth that was at this moment shaped in an O as she regarded me with unabashed schoolgirl surprise.

Lawrence performed the introductions and I performed my "how-d'ye-dos" with creditable grace. Lucinda responded prettily in a high, breathless voice. She seemed discomfited, probably because of my age. I could not be more than three years her senior.

The moment we had all seated ourselves, Lady Applecroft immediately launched into speech. "I was just telling Sir Lawrence, before your ladyship arrived, what a surprise he gave us all, wasn't I, Sir Henry?"

Her husband opened his mouth to reply, but Lady Applecroft continued, ignoring him. "Yes, indeed, you are a sly one, Sir Lawrence, and such a lovely bride, to be sure!" Her affable manner was belied for a brief instant as her gaze rested on me. She paused for breath before saying, "Why, I was just telling Sir Henry that we must pay our bridal visit. I said to Sir Henry just yesterday evening, didn't I?"

She looked momentarily at her husband, who barely managed to murmur, "Just so, my love," before she resumed her monologue.

"Yes, Sir Henry, I said, we must not let Sir Lawrence think we are backward in our attentions, so here we are, as you see!"

With that, she beamed at the entire company, patted her voluminous skirts, and settled back against the sofa.

I kept my mouth tightly closed, for I feared that I would giggle. There was a distinct twinkle in Lawrence's eye, but his voice was grave as he responded, "Her ladyship and I are most . . . grateful for your kind attention."

I marveled silently at his aplomb. John, on the other hand, leaned negligently against the mantel, looking like a man ready to be amused.

I soon discovered that a bridal visit cloaked Lady Applecroft's real reason for their call. After favoring us with her opinions on the weather and the condition of the roads, she paused a moment and cast a veiled look in John's direction. She tapped her fan on the vacant space beside her and beckoned John to her, saying archly, "John, you rogue, come and sit beside me!"

John straightened and walked lazily to the sofa and disposed himself comfortably beside her. Lady Applecroft leaned toward him and rapped his hand lightly with her fan, saying with affected severity, "Sir, you have not been to Blanford Hall for nearly a fortnight, and this silly puss here"—she indicated the blushing Lucinda—"asks me a dozen times a day if she asks me once, 'Where is John, Mama? Is John coming to dine, Mama?'"

"Oh, Mama, pray don't," begged, Lucinda, her color heightened prettily.

This maidenly display of blushing innocence gave way to a very coy, provocative look as Lucinda gazed at John through her lashes.

To my annoyance, I found myself thinking indignantly: Why, that schoolroom miss is flirting outrageously! As if a man of John's age and experience could be taken in by the blatant tactics of a scheming mama and that silly child!

To my surpirse, John did not at all appear to be annoyed or disgusted by the chit's behavior. On the contrary, he leaned over and possessed himself of one of Lucinda's small gloved hands and said in a most gallant and silky voice, "To behave so unfeelingly to such a charming young lady! I hope that I will be allowed to make reparations—very soon."

Lucinda's lashes fluttered most alluringly and her mouth formed a luscious pout. Lady Applecroft beamed and said in high good humour, "'Tis all settled, then. We will expect you to dinner tomorrow evening. We shall be a very gay company, I assure you, dear boy. Isn't that so, Sir Henry?"

"Certainly, my love," came the hurried reply.

Lucinda murmured coyly to John, "Indeed, sir, I would be most pleased if you began reparations tomorrow." Her voice lingered suggestively on "reparations."

John gave her a caressing smile.

Her mission accomplished, Lady Applecroft addressed

a few fleeting comments to Thomas, inquiring after his health, and then rose amid yards of rustling silk to take her leave. Lord Applecroft also rose hurridly. Lucinda stayed a moment longer, her head close to John's in further conversation. When she stood up finally and joined us, she was looking very pleased with herself.

How could John be taken in by such obvious tactics? I thought. Why, I continued to myself, if I had ever behaved in such a fashion, Grandfather would have boxed my ears! Oh, well, how John chose to conduct his flirts was certainly none of my affair. But something, a feeling I could not define, nagged at me, making my hands itch to shake the fair Lucinda and her matchmaking mama.

I managed to utter all the polite phrases required of my position. In the midst of their leave-taking, Lucinda suddenly turned her rapt attention from John to Lawrence and exclaimed in her breathless voice, "Sir Lawrence, you have not forgotten your promise?"

Lawrence looked down at her blankly for but a short moment before replying with amusement, "Of course I have not forgotten. If you will but jog my memory a bit, I will prove to you that I remember my promise all too well."

Lady Applecroft laughed gratingly and said in her strident voice, "Ah, Sir Lawrence, you are such a wit." Then, turning to her husband for seeming confirmation: "Haven't I told you many times, Sir Henry, that Sir Lawrence is always saying the drollest things?"

Called upon once again, Sir Henry replied enthusiastically, "Yes, indeed you have, my love!"

Lady Applecroft then tapped her daughter's arm lightly with her fan. "Now, don't tease his lordship, my pet." Her voice held no note of reproof.

Lawrence was looking vastly amused, and again addressed Lucinda. "Now, Lucinda, tell me about my promise."

In her breathless voice, a rosy blush coloring her cheeks, she said, "If you recall, Sir Lawrence, my coming out is in the spring. You promised that a ball here at Devbridge Manor would be just the thing to give me practice in meeting great people and, you know, in going on properly," she finished off in a rush. She gazed up at Lawrence with the same provocative look that she had earlier used on John.

Why, the little hussy, I thought, torn between amusement and annoyance.

Lawrence replied promptly, "Why, a most excellent promise, to be sure." He added thoughtfully, "And a formal ball would afford Lady Andrea the opportunity of meeting all our neighbors."

This aspect of the formal ball did not appeal to Lady Applecroft. In fact, I was fairly certain that my somewhat unexpected presence had caused her some discomfiture. But her face was quickly wreathed in smiles again as she nodded in enthusiastic agreement with my husband. After all, I was married and out of the way, as far as Lucinda was concerned.

Seeing my duty clear, and dearly loving to entertain besides, I turned to Lawrence and said, smiling, "My dear sir, it is indeed an excellent promise and I am most heartily in agreement." I thought of all the bedrooms in the west wing, long in disuse. This was indeed keeping my promise to myself to entertain as soon as possible.

Lucinda exclaimed, forgetting her breathless voice, "Oh, when, Sir Lawrence?"

Lawrence stroked his chin for a moment and then looked at me ruefully. "Let us see . . . how about the first week in December?"

I made rapid calculations. Nearly six weeks to send invitations, receive replies, make preparations. Yes, I could manage it.

"Yes, Lawrence, I believe that would be ample time."

"Very well. A ball it shall be," Lawrence said to Lucinda. She clapped her hands together excitedly, an action that reminded me forcibly of Judith.

The Applecrofts finally took their leave amid exclamations of delight from Lucinda and her mother. Sir Henry managed to take my hand and give it a squeeze. How impertinent of him, I thought indignantly. I removed my hand and gave him a cold stare.

As soon as Brantley had closed the doors after them, Lawrence turned to Amelia and said wryly, "Would you agree, Amelia, that Andrea has met our most . . . trying neighbors?"

"Odious, vulgar woman!" Amelia declared vehemently. She said in a mocking voice to John, "It appears that you have been totally taken in, dear brother."

John shrugged and replied indifferently, "Really, dear sister, one must have some diversions in the country."

I looked at him quickly, surprised at his total disregard for Lucinda's feelings. I said, "Really, John, do you think proper to take advantage, in so unfeeling a way . . . ?"

Lawrence held up his hand hastily, and said tactfully, "I think we need discuss the Applecrofts no further."

I frowned at John. He merely cocked an eye brow at me in seeming surprise.

"But really, Father," Amelia continued, "a ball for that chit?"

Lawrence shook his head. "Hardly, my dear. The ball is for Andrea; the Applecrofts will merely be guests with no special honors."

To my surprise, Amelia giggled. "The look on Lady Applecroft's face when she realized Andrea would preside at the ball!"

"By Jove, you're right, my love," chimed in Thomas. "She looked as though she'd swallowed a fish."

"Then she would be in excellent company, for her

husband, Sir Henry, must assuredly be one of the loosest fish I have yet to meet," I added.

"I hope he did not offend you, Andrea. I saw him press your hand over-long," Lawrence said.

"You should hear what he does with the house maid," John murmured.

Amelia went off into a peal of laughter.

"Does that mean I should count myself honored, John?" I retorted.

"Enough, enough," Lawrence interposed. "I think we have abused the topic sufficiently."

As each of us looked as if we would like to continue commenting on the Applecrofts, Lawrence hastily turned to John and asked, "Well, my boy, how was your ride this morning?"

My eyes flew to John's face. He met my gaze for but a moment before replying blandly to his father, "It was a very . . . enlightening experience."

I wanted very much to box his ears. I opened my mouth to say something, when John continued smoothy, "You are right, sir, Andrea in an excellent horsewoman."

Then he added maliciously, giving me a quick glance, "My most heartfelt sympathies for her poor groom. He will undoubtedly break his neck trying to keep up with her!"

"Sir," I exclaimed, "John . . . exaggerates. In truth, we had a most uneventful ride." I glared meaningfully at John.

"Uneventful . . . good lord." John smiled wickedly.

Before Lawrence could unravel this, Thomas said with considerable surprise, "Ho, what's this, John? You approving a female whip?"

"Alas, brother, even I must occasionally modify my opinions," John said mournfully.

Lawrence chuckled. He turned to me. "That is quite a concession from John, my dear."

Thomas declared, "I think he's brought brain fever back from the army, that's what I think!"

"Tut, tut," John said blandly. "You are undermining the lady's skill, brother."

With that he walked lazily to the door, turned, and tossed over his shoulder, "I think it is time for luncheon."

My lips twitched. You are indeed a devil, Master Jack, I thought.

Lawrence looked questioningly from one to the other of us. Amelia rose, yawned delicately behind a white hand, and said in the voice of one sorely tried, "I agree with John. It is time for luncheon. This talk of female whips and brain fever is quite fatiguing and most out-of-place in the drawing room."

"'A most acute observation, my dear sister," John said mockingly as he proffered her his arm and led her out of the room.

"Quite right, quite right, my love," Thomas called after her. "Not at all the thing for the drawing room!"

FIVE

The days sped by and melted into weeks. As the newness and strangeness of my surroundings gradually faded, I began to settle into my own routine. In the mornings I would normally spend a half-hour with Mrs. Eliott, reviewing the menu for dinner and discussing any domestic problems that she felt I should be concerned with. Since the domestic problems scarce ever concerned anything more important than a darned sheet, my house-wifely skills were not taxed.

Mrs. Eliott herself remained somewhat of a mystery to me. She was invariably stiff, rigid, and unbending both in her physical demeaner and in her speech. Any questions or comments I addressed to her were answered in a mono-syllable. She became expansive only on those occassions when I asked her questions about the family history. On this topic she would wax eloquent. One day, when we were in the long gallery. I asked her why there was no portrait of the second Countess of Devbridge, Lady Caroline. Her eyes held mine for a brief moment, an expression in them that I could not read, and then darted away, looking at a point beyond my face. In her precise voice she said, "His lordship commissioned an artist, but her ladyship became too . . . ill for the sittings." Then abruptly she said, "If your ladyship will excuse me." She walked away after I nodded, her black silk skirt swaying gracefully. I frowned after her for a moment, wondering at her odd behavior. It seemed that any questions to do with Lady Caroline or the Blue Room were upsetting to Mrs. Eliott. I wondered why. I turned back to look at the portraits of the present earl's family. Poor Lady Caroline, I thought, such a tragedy. Would my portrait be painted, I wondered, as the third Countess of Devbridge?

I was to think of the unfortunate Lady Caroline each time I leaned out of my window, for the holes that were her prison bars were a grim reminder.

The summer weather held for those weeks, and I spent several hours each morning riding Dante. We were great friends now and Dante would acknowledge this with a toss of his head and a snort of welcome each time that I saw him. Sometimes I rode with Lawrence, and twice with John. I accompanied Thomas upon several occasions to inspect improvements being made on tenant cottages. Amelia, no rider, occasionally sallied forth in the gig.

As John had maliciously predicted, I was a sad trial to Billy, my groom, for when it became apparent that a sedate canter along well-marked paths was not to my liking, Billy found himself in a quandary. He tried gallantly to at least keep me in view. When this failed, I would find him waiting for me, muttering dark predictions under his breath. I would laugh and beg him not to go on so. Even if I rode alone, I reasoned with him, what could possibly happen to me? But Billy, a staunch believer in the fraility of womankind, continued to shake his head and mutter under his breath.

A favorite part of my day was the hours I spent with Judith and Miss Gillbank in the early afternoons. When the weather permitted, we walked in the garden, tossed Judith's bright ball back and forth on the front lawn, or took a picnic lunch to the lake. Judith would skip along ahead of us down the path through the home woods while Miss Gillbank and I gradually eased into a comfortable friendship. The day finally came when I begged her most heartily to call me Andrea, for "my lady" and "your ladyship" sounded strange on her lips and created differences between us that were restrictive.

"Besides, after saying all that, one is likely to forget the point of one's conversation," I added.

She smiled and said in her easy way, "Very well, but you must call me Sophy." Then she laughed aloud. "Miss Gillbank does sound like a prim and proper person, does it not?"

I agreed, smiling. We were both chuckling when Judith appeared suddenly from behind a bush to surprise us. She instantly demanded to know about our joke. Sophy replied, "Her ladyship, or rather, Andrea and I were just talking about prim-and-proper governesses."

Judith screwed up her face in a grimace and exclaimed, "I'm glad you're not like that, Gilly."

"Judith," Sophy declared in mock reproof, "you must remember my dignity. Gilly sounds like a pet kitten!"

Judith laughed in delight and appeared impressed by such a quaint comparison.

When it rained, we ate luncheon in the schoolroom and I would sit with Judith during her Italian lesson. One day Judith informed me with childish frankness, "I like you best, Andrea, after Gilly, of course . . . even though you are Father's wife."

Evenings at Devbridge Manor also settled into a comfortable routine. Gradually Amelia came to accept Sophy's presence at the dinner table with at least civility.

After dinner, if music or conversation was not desired, Lawrence and I would play chess or take turns making up the fourth at whist. Sophy, in particular, was a skilled player and invariably won. When Amelia cut Sophy for a partner, she was more than just civil. Sophy seemed to take all this in stride, her friendly, open manners never varying.

John, true to his promise to Lucinda, was absent on several evenings at dinner. One evening upon his return from the Applecrofts', he was in the blackest of moods. I grinned to myself, thinking of Lady Applecroft's incessant chatter. It serves him right, I thought, harking back to his outrageous behavior the morning of the Applecrofts' first visit. Amelia roasted him roundly, pointing out that sometimes diversions in the country were not preferable to quiet evenings spent in the bosom of one's family.

"Dashed if Amelia isn't right, John," Thomas chimed in. "The old harpy fairly got her hooks into you, that's for sure!"

I added maliciously, "Well, you know, Thomas, some people are so easily taken in. Why, all you have to do is flatter them and they fairly jump to the bait."

Unjustly, John rounded on me. "Flatter . . . flatter!" he exclaimed, his face a thundercloud.

I burst out laughing, for John was at a loss for words for the first time since I had known him.

Lawrence intervened with severity. "Enough, all of you! John has had, understandably, a trying evening." Frowning at each of us in turn, he added, "I defy any of you to spend the evening in Lady Applecroft's company without returning in a raving depression."

"I am sorry, John," I said meekly after a few moments of silence. "I am quite certain that I, too, would be in a raving depression, that is, of course, if I would ever willingly put myself in such a position."

John shot me a look of acute dislike, said clipped good nights to our assembled company, and departed to bed.

Lawrence chided, "Really, Andrea, you should not mock him so."

Surprisingly, Amelia exclaimed, "'Oh, no, Father, it was so funny. 'Twill do John good to get a taste of his own medicine."

I did apologize to John later about the remarks I had made that evening. He looked blankly at me and then frowned. I realized that he hadn't remembered what I was talking about. Finally he replied indifferently, "Oh, that. Don't tease yourself further. It was, after all, a good joke."

I saw John less frequently as the weeks sped by. It seemed to me at times as if he were purposely avoiding my company. I could find no reason why John should be angry with me, for I had apologized.

During those weeks my relationship with my husband became more and more like that of an indulgent father with a favorite child. Lawrence showered me with little gifts, and some gifts that were not trifles. He bestowed the Devbridge emeralds on me with much pomp one evening. He was invariably kind, even when I was in the wrong, and made no demands upon me in any way. He would brush his lips lightly against my cheek each night before he left me to Belinda. I was not so naive as to suppose that there was love between us. I held him in esteem. His feelings to me, I could not guess. Perhaps my youth and liveliness had attracted him, for he could have no interest in my fortune, being a wealthy man. Sometimes I wondered if perhaps he had owed some sort of obligation to Grandfather. In any case, I accepted our arrangement and tried to please him, or at the very least, not to displease him. I had decided soon after our marriage that I must take each day as it came, for I did not have the courage to look into the future. And, I reasoned, my present life was as I had wished it to be. Any nagging doubts or unwanted thoughts and feelings I kept resolutely out of my mind.

As the day for the ball grew nearer, the manor began to bustle with activity. The servants unearthed and washed hundreds of plates and glasses. The floor of the huge ballroom at the back of the manor was scrubbed and polished to a rich shine. The chandeliers were polished until the glass sparkled like hundreds of twinkling jewels. The heavy brocade draperies covering the tall windows were taken down and beaten until all the accumulated dust of at least five years floated to the ground.

All the bedrooms in the west wing were dusted and holland covers packed away. As acceptances arrived, Amelia help me decide which guests would stay in what bedroom, all the while giving me the latest *on dits* about certain ladies and gentlemen that I did not know.

I asked Lawrence if we could not have the musicians who had played for my coming-out ball, as I had loved their way with the waltz. Smiling indulgently, he agreed, seemingly pleased and amused with my headlong plunge into the preparations.

One morning, about three days before the ball and the day before we were expecting the first of our London guests to arrive, I was interrupted at my breakfast by Mrs. Eliott bearing the mail. I had arranged with Lawrence to receive the mail so that I could quickly take care of acceptances.

Mrs. Eliott excused herself and handed me a salver with an array of envelopes on it. I began to look negligently through them as I sipped my coffee. I exclaimed in surprised delight when I saw an envelope with Peter's familiar handwriting.

Mrs. Eliott turned at the door and asked, "Is anything wrong, my lady?"

"Oh, no, Mrs. Eliott. It is just that I have received my first letter from my brother. 'Tis a pleasant surprise."

She gave a brief curtsy and left the room. I ripped open the envelope and pulled out a sheet of paper covered with Peter's scrawl. Beside his letter was another folded sheet of paper. I put it aside for the moment. Smoothing out the sheet, I read:

4 November, 1818

My dearest sister,

I hope my letter finds you well. I will not bore you with life in Brussels. Indeed, the express reason for writing is to assure you of my regard and concern and to enclose a letter from Father. It is Father's handwriting; of that I can attest, even though I have not seen it for years. I know this will be a shock to you, Andrea, but I beg you to read it with an open mind. I feel his concern to be real, even though he does not explain his reasons. I am leaving Brussels as soon as possible and hope to be with you by Christmas. Take care, Drea.

Your devoted brother,

Peter

I sat there rigid for a moment. A letter from Father! I stared at the folded piece of paper at my hand. After all these years, he was coming back into my life. Grandfather had refused even to mention his name after my mother's death, but I had heard a short time later that he had disappeared, had left England to make his home somewhere on the Continent.

My hand trembled as I touched the paper, and a wave

of bitterness flooded over me, bitterness and anger. How dare he try to come back into my life after he had left me, without a word, so many years ago!

I felt a strong desire to rip his letter to shreds, but Peter's message was a mystery, and to solve that mystery I had to read Father's letter.

I unfolded the paper and began to read the unfamiliar, sloping handwriting.

My dear daughter,

I did not write you directly for fear that this letter would not reach your hand or that you would refuse to read it. This is why I wrote to your brother. Please, my child, listen to what I have to say to you. I, of course, read of your marriage to the Earl of Devbridge and was stunned and shocked. It is not the difference in your ages, but something else, something you would not understand.

Please, Andrea, do as I ask now. Flee Devbridge Manor while you still have time. You are not safe. Trust no one. Believe that I shall not be idle.

Your father,

Edward Branyon Jameson

Flee Devbridge Manor? I was not safe! Why, what arrant nonsense! I curled my lip in anger. Did he think he could take me in with obscure rantings? But Peter believed him. I frowned and reread the scrawled lines, lines obviously written in much agitation and haste.

I sat back in my chair and tried to detach myself from the violent feelings I felt for this man, my father. As I became more calm, I began to wonder if my father were mad, so incoherent and rambling was his letter. But Peter did not appear to think him mad. Again I subjected the letter to close scrutiny, trying to make sense of it, to understand. Answers to my questions did not come from the third or the fourth reading. Why should I be threatened at Devbridge Manor? Who would wish to harm me? Suddenly an answer to that question rose to my eyes like a terrible vision that had been waiting to be called up. The old woman! She had wanted to kill me! Or had she?

I shook my head, unable to unravel my thoughts. I looked down at my father's letter again. What did my father know of the Earl of Devbridge? What was it that I would not understand? "Oh, the devil!" I muttered in frustration. For one moment I determined to show the letter to my husband, but something inside me made me dismiss this idea.

This is all fantastic, I thought, shaking my head in confusion. I rose quickly from my chair and walked to the large windows. Warm sunlight poured into the room. I stood motionless, gazing out onto the east lawn. One of the gardeners was scything the grass. Two peacocks strolled lazily and conceitedly toward the small rock garden. The scene before my eyes was so normal, so calm, so real that the mere thought of something or someone sinister or malevolent was laughable. I was not safe here? I shook my head in pity at my father's ravings. He would have me trust him? I would never trust or willingly see the man who had killed my mother, the man who had disappeared from my life, leaving only hurt and death!

Peter had been taken in, I decided. Why, he must have been, to ask to be relieved of his obligations to Lord Brooke and be back in England by Christmas!

I folded both letters back into the envelope and slipped it inside my bodice.

Later I placed the envelope in an elegantly carved lacquered box that Peter had given me one Christmas and locked the lid. Something stopped me as I opened my dresser drawer to drop the key inside. For some reason unknown to myself, I took a pin instead and fastened the small golden key to my chemise.

As I lay in bed that night, my mind drifted back to the letters. My fingers went to the key that now hung on a golden chain around my neck. I began to feel somewhat ridiculous for having taken such pains. The more I thought about Father's letter, the more convinced I became that he was either mad or trying in some strange way to reestablish himself in my affections. I wondered cynically if he were in need of funds. I resolved to put the matter out of my mind.

Our guests arrived throughout the morning on the next day. For the time being, at least, I was able to forget about my father's letter, for being a hostess took all my time and energies. My day was spent quite happily in dispensing tea, engaging in idle conversation, encouraging fatigued ladies to rest from the tiring journeys and making sure the gentlemen were provided with ample port, playing cards, and cigars. Both Amelia and John showed themselves in a new light. They enjoyed themselves immensely, as did I, laughing and joking and entertaining our guests in high style. I looked up from my own conversations several times at the sound of John's deep full laughter. He looked like a different person when he laughed, I thought, for his eyes laughed too.

The evening was spent in more gossip, card playing, and musical performances. Much to my dislike, I was talked into playing the pianoforte. The young Duc de Chaillon, who had attached himself to me the entire day, begged to turn my pages. Acquiescing, I chose two Scottish tunes. As I sang the haunting, tragic words of love to our most untragic audience, the duke leaned against the pianoforte and gazed at me pointedly. Lawrence teased me about my conquest, saying that I would most probably receive passionate declarations of love from our noble visitor. I returned dryly that our noble duke undoubtedly felt secure conducting a light flirtation with a married lady. Lawrence just shook his head in amusement at my rejoinder, pinched my cheek, and told me I was much too modest. I was left to fend off the young duke for the remainder of the evening, for Lawrence adjourned to the library with several of the gentlemen to play piquet.

The morning of the ball dawned clear but rather cool. I was up and dressed quite early, too excited to sleep. I was at the breakfast table with only one other hardy lady discussing the latest fashions from Paris when a footman entered and informed me that two boxes had just arrived by special messenger from London. I gulped down the remainder of my coffee and hurriedly excused myself.

I arrived at the front hall in time to hear the special messenger endeavoring to justify his delay in arrival to Brantley. Brantley gave this inferior person to understand that he, Brantley, would now see to the matter.

Brantley turned and bowed to me. "My lady, I understand that these packages are from Madame Lavaubier, your modiste in London."

"Yes, Brantley," I affirmed. I turned and thanked the messenger and directed him to the servants' hall for refreshment after his tiring journey.

A few moments later in the Ladies' Parlour I was excitedly pulling off the wrapping paper. Nestled in the boxes were the two ball gowns that I had ordered. One was for me and the other for Sophy. I lifted Sophy's gown from its box and gazed at it in delight. It was an exquisite pale gold silk with a tightly fitted bodice and an overskirt of darker gold gauze. It would become Sophy's slender figure to perfection, I thought. I knew that the gown would fit, for Belinda had taken the proper measurements. I wrapped the gown carefully back into the silver tissue, quickly sat down and wrote her a formal invitation, and finally, box and invitation in hand, I made my way to Sophy's room. She answered my knock, a startled look on her face.

"Why, what a surprise, my . . . Andrea," she exclaimed. "Do come in," she added, stepping aside for me to enter.

"Thank you," I replied as I handed her the invitation to the dinner and to the ball. As she read the invitation, her look of surprise changed into one of distress. After a moment she said quietly, "How very kind you are, Andrea, but you must know that this is not at all the thing. It is, in fact, impossible."

"But why, Sophy?" I asked swiftly.

She smiled slightly, but her voice trembled. "There are two very sound reasons. First, I am Judith's governess. My presence at your ball would cause comment, Andrea. That you must surely recognize. It could lead to embarrassment."

"Sophy, that is ridiculous and you know it," I cried roundly. "Now, what is your second very sound reason?"

"Very well, but you cannot term this reason ridiculous. You must know that I have nothing suitable to wear for such a grand occasion."

I gave a cry of delight and whipped the box from behind my back. "Oh, yes, you do, Miss Gillbank. Oh, Sophy, I wanted to ask you sooner, but your dress is but just this minute arrived from London. And if you must know, I was afraid that if I did not have the dress, you would refuse me for sure."

Sophy looked stupefied as she took the box from my hands and carried it to her bed. Almost mechanically she unwrapped the tissue and lifted the gown from the box and stared at it blankly.

"It is so beautiful," she murmured as she ran her fingers over the soft material.

"And it is yours, Sophy. I ordered it made especially for you," I said happily.

With that, she stiffened and turned to me, tears glistening in her eyes. "Your ladyship is too kind, but of course I cannot accept such an expensive gift." Her voice was rigid. I had unintentionally offended her.

For a moment I did not know how to respond. I had made a mull of it and hurt the one person at Devbridge Manor who was truly my friend. I crossed to her and laid my hand on her arm.

"Please, Sophy," I begged. "I meant no offense. You cannot think that I would . . ." I ground to a halt, unable to continue, not knowing what to say.

Almost immediately she clasped my hand and said warmly, "Forgive me, Andrea. I'm such a beast . . . of course you meant only to be kind. You are a dear friend."

I wanted to interrupt, but she continued in her calm voice, "But surely you must see that I cannot accept your kindness."

I recovered myself and said with severity, "For goodness' sake, Sophy, my so-called kindness can go to the devil! You know I don't care a fig for all that nonsense, and I would very much enjoy having my best friend attend my ball."

She smiled, but there was still doubt written on her face.

I continued quickly, not giving her time to muster further arguments.

"I knew you would refuse, had I asked you, and you know quite well, Sophy, that you would not have had the opportunity to order a new gown. I want you so much to come to my first ball, Sophy!" My words tumbled over each other so that by the time I had finished, they had come out in a breathless rush.

Sophy was silent for a moment. Her face was a study in conflicting emotions. Finally she squeezed my hand and said in a tremulous voice, "You are a dear, thoughtful person, Andrea, and I do accept your invitation."

There was a light tap on the door, followed by an impetuous entrance by Judith.

"Oh, hello, Andrea. What are you doing here?" she inquired, surprised.

Sophy replied gaily, "Andrea is helping Cinderella to prepare for the ball."

Judith came skipping into the room. She gave an "oh" of delight as Sophy held the gown in front of her and began to waltz around the room.

"Is it not a beautiful gown, poppet?" Sophy held out the gown for Judith to touch.

"You will be a fairy princess," Judith cried. "But you cannot be Cinderella, Gilly, for you are a governess, not a chimney sweep!"

"Quite true," replied Sophy, laughing. "That was a most inaccurate comparison, and you, my child, are altogether too precocious!"

Judith sighed and said wistfully, "I wish I were old enough to come."

Sophy put the gown down on the bed, put her arms around Judith, and then tousled her fair hair. She said gently, "Ah, Judith, 'twill be such a short time when we shall be putting your hair up and getting you ready for your first ball. You'll see, poppet. It will all come too soon." She looked up at me and smiled.

"Speaking of getting ready, Sophy, I shall send Belinda to you this evening."

She spoke hastily. "Surely I can manage for myself, Andrea."

I replied, teasing, "You are indeed a wizard, Miss Gillbank, but the dozens of tiny buttons are beyond even your reach!"

Sophy peered at the buttons and then nodded ruefully.

I added, putting on an affected accent, "And, my dear, you cannot expect such an august company to be satisfied with anything less than the most elegant of coiffures."

Sophy flung up her hands, saying in mock capitulation, "I am quite vanquished and find myself totally in your hands."

I then realized the time. "Oh, dear," I exclaimed, "it is I who will be vanquished if I do not go and see to the wants of our guests."

I turned and said over my shoulder as I reached the door, "I have seated you next to Lord Applecroft at dinner. I only pray that he will not pinch your knee."

"If he dares," Sophy quickly retorted, "I shall contrive to spill wine on his waistcoat."

"That will put him in full retreat, for he is such a dandy." I laughed.

"As for you, Judith," I added, smiling at her, "I shall make sure that cook sends you at least two apple tarts."

Judith's bright blue eyes shone at this pleasing prospect.

Later in the afternoon, after a light luncheon, most of the ladies retired to their rooms to rest and prepare for the evening's festivities. I had no desire to rest, for I was filled with nervous excitement. I made my way first to the kitchen and checked cook's progress with dinner. I had planned an elaborate selection of dishes designed to please the most exacting of palates. After complimenting the flushed Mrs. Meldorson and the kitchen staff on their excellent work, I went in search of my husband. Brantley informed me in discouraging tones that his lordship was in the billiard room with several of the gentlemen. Well aware that I could not invade the gentlemen's stronghold, I decided to take a brisk walk in the garden. I wrapped a light shawl around my shoulders and made my way out of the back of the manor. As I strolled from one lane into another, thinking excitedly of the evening to come, I chanced to hear conversation from one of the side lanes. Curious, I peered around the bushes to see who was there. John and Lady Elizabeth Torrington were seated on a bench beneath one of the overhanging rose arbors, their heads close together in intimate conversation. I drew back instantly, my body rigid. A strange feeling of sadness and pain shot through me, and I had an unaccountable urge to cry. I bit my lips until I felt physical pain. This pain, at least, I could understand and deal with rationally. I turned quickly and began retracing my steps, when I heard John's deep, full laugh. I turned around in spite of myself, to see his dark head bent close to Lady Elizabeth's face. I fancied that I could see her brilliant green eyes flash with pleasure. I gave what I told myself was an indifferent shrug and hurried noiselessly away. I knew very little of Lady Elizabeth. I had thought her insufferably proud and condescending during our brief exchange of civilities upon her arrival the previous day. She was one of the leaders of London society and a beautiful woman with bright, almost flaming auburn hair and vivid green eyes. Her figure was voluptuous, I thought bitterly, and her tongue sharp. I had seen her many times during my first Season in London, but a young miss was hardly worthy of her attention. She had bestowed upon me only the scantest of notice. It was common knowledge that Lord Torrington did not much concern himself with his lady's many activities. In fact, he had not accompanied her here. Amelia had insisted that she be invited, and now that I thought of it, John had echoed his total agreement. Was John one of her amours? I wondered bitterly. Why, John was just like my father—an unprincipled libertine! First Lucinda, and now Lady Elizabeth, a married woman. They deserved each other, I thought angrily. I consigned both John and the beautiful Lady Elizabeth to the devil. I was shocked at the intensity of my feelings, and at the thought of the unwitting comparison I had made between John and my father, I broke into a run.

I made my way to the Ladies' Parlour, away from all the guests, until I could regain my calm. I thought wryly that the Ladies' Parlour had become my refuge. A short time later, my feelings under better control, I entered the formal dining room to make a final inspection of the table. Thirty-eight covers had been laid. Magnificent flower arrangements were placed at intervals down the long table. I happened to glance down at the name cards, and in a gesture of childish revenge I seated John next to Lady Applecroft and placed Lady Elizabeth between old Colonel Bridestow and Lucinda Applecroft. There, I thought maliciously, that should keep John and Lady Elizabeth properly entertained!

For the remainder of the afternoon I most willingly and gratefully placed myself in Belinda's capable hands. She dressed my hair simply but elegantly high atop my head with two thick curls falling to my shoulder. She gave an "Ooh" of delight as she fastened my gown of pomona-green silk and smoothed down the yards of lace trimming. Satisfied with my appearance as the new

Countess of Devbridge, I made my way down to greet our guests in the drawing room.

They formed a glittering company and were all in high spirits. The Duc de Chaillon claimed my attention until Brantley, at his most dignified, announced dinner. As we filed through the Old Hall to the dining room, I noticed that John was leading Lady Elizabeth. Well, John, I thought, my jaw tightening, you will not be in her company for very long!

Dinner was a success, and I silently blessed Mrs. Meldorson and the kitchen staff as course after course was served by silent footmen. I was slowly sipping a glass of wine when I happened to look down the table at Lady Elizabeth. Her lustrous auburn hair was piled artfully on top of her head, and she looked cold and unapproachable. The poor Lucinda looked quite subdued seated next to such an illustrious personage. My eyes traveled to where John was seated. Lady Applecroft had a firm hold on his attention, and he looked unutterably bored. I knew that his inbred civility would not permit him to be rude. John looked up, and our eyes held for a brief moment. He raised his wineglass in a silent toast toward me. His eyes smoldered angrily, and I felt a dull flush creep over my cheeks. He knew what I had done and was obviously furious. I gave my head a toss and turned to my dinner partner.

The gentlemen did not indulge in their customary glass of port and cigars at the end of dinner. Lawrence gave me a signal, and we both rose together.

As Lawrence led me onto the floor for the first waltz, I noticed from the corner of my eye that the Duc de Chaillon had possessed himself of Sophy's hand. She looked quite beautiful, her golden gown shimmering in the soft candlelight.

Lawrence smiled down at me and said, "Our Sophy, it appears, has made a conquest." His eyes followed the graceful couple as they whirled in wide circles around the ballroom.

"How fickle you men are," I said mournfully.

Lawrence grinned. "You are doing an admirable job, madam, of hiding your broken heart."

Later in the evening, after a particularly fast waltz, I escaped my partner and retreated to a partially opened window at the end of the ballroom. I was leaning against the casement fanning myself when I heard John say from behind me, "I believe the musicians are striking up another waltz. Would you care to dance, ma'am?"

I stiffened. I had avoided him all evening, chattering with whoever was closest to me whenever he came near to me. I slowly turned around and replied stiffly, my eyes fastened on the top button of his waistcoat, "Forgive me, sir, but I have already promised this dance to Lord Brasham."

"Then he is a lowly fellow indeed, for I just this moment saw him solicit the hand of Lucinda Applecroft."

My eyes flew to his face.

He continued smoothly, "Surely, my dear, I cannot be that distasteful a partner. I do not recall having trod upon a lady's toes these past five years."

Caught in such a stupid lie, I could not meet his steady gaze, nor could I think of anything to say. Realizing he was in full control of the situation, John possessed himself of my hand and led me onto the dance floor. He slipped his arm easily around my waist and began to whirl me around in wider and wider circles. I kept my head down, unwilling to engage in conversation. After a few moments he finally slowed to a more sedate pace.

"I cannot believe that the buttons on my waistcoat can be so fascinating," he said conversationally.

I looked up at him. He was smiling down at me sardonically, his even teeth gleaming very white against his dark countenance.

He continued blandly, "Now, madam, that I have you in a secured position and have drawn your attention from my waistcoat, you will be so kind as to explain the unfortunate mixup of dinner partners."

My mind was working frantically. I could not admit to what I had done, for to do so would leave me vulnerable to more questions about my motives. Taking a deep breath, I returned in an equally bland voice, "Really, sir, I have not the slightest notion of what you are talking about!"

His arm tightened perceptibly around my waist. "Oh, do you not, madam? Strive to jog your lamentably short memory!"

I did not reply, but simply thrust my chin higher and stared up at him defiantly.

The gleaming smile was still on his face, and he continued quite conversationally, "Tell me, sweet Andrea, what great offense did I commit to be so placed at dinner? Lady Applecroft, indeed!"

My courage was sinking rapidly, but I still managed to reply in a fairly composed voice, "Really, John, you must know—in fact, you just this moment alluded to it yourself—that seating arragnements can very easily become . . . misarranged."

"A churlish trick, my dear. Perhaps the same misarrangement accounted for Lady Elizabeth's being placed between Lucinda Applecroft and old Bridestow?"

I could think of nothing to say. I was at fault, but I could not bring myself to try to explain my actions. It would sound fantastic!

The sarcastic tone continued. "I had no idea that you would be an . . . interfering stepmama."

Stung, I tried to pull away from him, but his arm tightened. Realizing that I could not get away from him and that I could not continue with my denials, I said in a small voice, "Very well, John, it was I. Please accept my apologies. It was an unkind thing to have done. I meant it only as a . . . joke." Even to my own ears, my explanation sounded false and stupidly lame.

He seemed to relax his hold on me, and said in a milder voice, "But why, Andrea, did you pull such a trick?"

I looked up into his face, into the depths of his dark blue eyes. There was a slight catch in my throat as I repeated, "It was but a joke, really."

I heard him say, as if from a distance, "You are such a pathetic liar." Then, unexpectedly: "I do wish you would tell me the truth."

His deep blue eyes pierced into mine. I must get away, away from him, I thought wildly. Again I felt an unaccountable urge to cry. But instead, I replied in a voice so full of bitterness and sadness that I did not recognize it as my own. "I saw you and Lady Elizabeth this afternoon in the garden. You were making love to her. I could not believe that you an-and . . ." I stammered to a halt and shook my head, trying to come out of this nightmare, to break his hold on me.

He pursued inexorably, continuing my thought for me, "Yes, that I and the Lady Elizabeth should what, Andrea? What?"

The truth came tumbling out in a strangled, bitter whisper. "That you would desire another woman . . . no, no, it is not that," I cried, trying to save myself. "I mean, desire a married woman! I cannot bear that you be like my father . . . it is unspeakable!"

John's brows flew up and he gazed down at me intently. I could not read his expression. Before he could speak, the enormity of what I had said flooded me and I felt such shame and such embarrassment that I could no longer bear it. I tried to jerk free from him, but he held me fast.

"Let me go. Please let me go," I begged in a broken voice.

"Remember your position, my lady," he said in a cool voice. "There are many here who would positively dote on such interesting actions."

His coldness steadied me, as well as the truth of what he said. Mechanically, like a puppet, I allowed him to lead me until the waltz ended. When it did, John held my held in a firm grasp and said softly, "We must speak of this again, Andrea."

I pulled my hand away, turned, and put the distance of the long ballroom between us. I felt the telltale flush creep over my face, but inside I felt coldness and a numbing pain.

"Why, Andrea, are you all right?" Lawrence's kind voice sounded at my elbow.

In a voice that sounded too bright and too high, I replied, "Why, of course, Lawrence. We are quite a success tonight, are we not?"

"Indeed we are." He sensed my agitation, so I turned quickly away and addressed the dowager Duchess of Wiggan.

I avoided John for the remainder of the evening and threw all my energies into being a vivacious and entertaining hostess. Because the majority of our guests were staying at the manor, the ball continued until well after three o'clock in the morning.

When I finally tumbled into bed, I was thankful for my physical exhaustion, for it helped quiet my jumbled thoughts.

I was finally at the point of drifting into sleep when suddenly I jerked up in my bed. I realized that I had forgotten to lock my door after the sleepy Belinda had left. During the day, my nightly ritual seemed silly, but at night, alone, my fears returned. Trembling from the cold as well as from my fear, I padded quickly across the carpet to the door. As my eyes became accustomed to the darkness, I forced myself to peer around my room looking into every corner, examining every shadow. There was nothing. Heaving a sigh of relief, I slowly opened the door to look into the corridor. At first, I could only make out the seemingly endless expanse of hallway. But suddenly there was a pale shaft of light and a shadow. I heard the light rustling of movement. My first impulse was to close my door as quickly as possible and lock it. I fought with my cowardly self for several moments before making the convincing argument that I was no longer alone in the west wing, that, in fact, almost every chamber was occupied. Thus equipped with sound reason, I stepped noiselessly into the hallway. Far down the hall I could make out the outline of a woman wearing a long, loose gown. I tiptoed after her. The woman glided quickly down the hall and stopped, turned around, and tapped lightly upon a door. When the door opened but a moment later, a shaft of light illuminated the scene. It was Lady Elizabeth, her long auburn hair flowing over a flimsy dressing gown. She reached out her arms seductively and embraced the man in the doorway. I saw a dark head bend down over her face. A sob caught in my throat. Although I could not make out the man clearly, I felt it must be John.

I turned and ran soundlessly back to my room. Locking the door, I crossed quickly to my bed. The mountains of warm covers did not stop my violent shivering. Unwanted tears stung my eyes and rolled heedlessly down my cheeks. In a blinding flash of truth I knew that I was afraid to truly examine my feelings, for I knew what they were. I loved John. I loved him though he was like my father. I was a weak fool, like my mother, I realized bitterly. I began pounding my fists against the pillows, raging against my feelings, against fate. After a few moments I began to feel calmer. I must not allow myself to continue thinking or feeling this way, or I would be the unhappiest of women. No, I must think of my husband, of his kindness and gentleness and of my new life, the life I had myself chosen. In spite of my logical reasoning, I remained tortured and miserable. Finally exhausted, I fell into a fitful sleep.

I awoke the next morning with a pounding headache and my face blotched from my crying. If Belinda noticed, she said nothing, but merely helped me apply rather more powder than usual. I dreaded going downstairs for fear of seeing John or Lady Elizabeth. To my surprise and puzzlement, I arrived in time only to wish Lady Elizabeth, Lord Brasham, the Duc de Chaillon, and several other guests good-bye. The Duc explained, as he bowed elegantly over my hand, that he was called back to London and must leave, regretfully, immediately. Lady Elizabeth proffered no explanation, and despite my curiosity, I could not inquire.

The remainder of our guests lingered up to a week after the ball, making their visit to Devbridge Manor the first in their rounds of Christmas parties. During that week I had no great difficulty in avoiding John, for most of my time was spent in planning delectable meals with Mrs. Eliott, chattering amiably with the ladies and gentlemen, and planning evening entertainments. In a way, I regretted the departure of our guests, for the many plans and activities kept me from dwelling overmuch upon my own feelings.

Our first evening without guests, our conversation lagged and spirits were low. Lawrence and I settled into a game of chess after dinner, and the others joined to play halfheartedly at whist.

Lawrence seemed preoccupied, his mind obviously not on the game. I set a trap to check his King and to win his Queen, a kind of tactic that would normally be recognized and rebuffed instantly. But tonight he failed to see the maneuver and lost his Queen. A few moves later he was forced to resign. He sat back, stared at the board for a moment, and then shook his head, a rueful smile on his lips. "Very well played, my dear," he finally said softly.

"Nonsense," I said lightly. "You were not attending at all to the game. I fear that your mind is many miles away, Lawrence. Perhaps with our departed guests?"

"Perhaps. But in any event, I am poor company for you this evening," he replied, sighing.

"We are all suffering from the doldrums after the excitement of this past week," I said as I gathered the chess pieces together and put them away.

Competition over the game of whist seemed not to have been too fierce, for there were no arguments or recriminations when we gathered together for tea. Our party broke up shortly after tea, each drifting languidly off to bed.

Lawrence, as was his custom, escorted me to my room. We stood a moment before the door to the Blue Room, and I waited to receive his light kiss on my cheek. Instead, he cupped my chin in his hand and lifted my face to his. He said in almost a melancholy voice, "Our game of chess was most interesting tonight, was it not?"

I cocked my head slightly, looking at him questioningly.

"What I meant was that one should never underestimate one's opponent," he added, smiling down into my face.

Wondering if his poorly played game had made him feel bad, I quickly said, "Oh, pooh, Lawrence. Whatever can one silly game of chess mean?"

"Of course, you are quite right, my dear," he said softly after a moment. He leaned down, kissed my cheek, turned, and walked away.

I stood silently for a moment, looking after him wonderingly.

As Belinda helped me to change into my nightgown, she looked several times toward the windows and sniffed the air. "A mighty storm be coming soon," she announced finally. "But listen, my lady," she continued as she motioned me over to the window, "the wind is rising sharp now."

Belinda's prediction proved accurate. Shortly after midnight, it seemed as though the elements conspired to plunge us into winter. Rain fell in torrents, bowing the trees, while violent winds lashed branches against the windows and made the casements groan in protest. I slept soundly in spite of the storm, for I was well used to the unpredictable and many times violent weather in Yorkshire.

During my breakfast the next morning I kept looking out the windows to see if the rain had stopped. Unfortunately, it continued, and I heaved a sigh of disappointment, for I had not ridden Dante for several days and was restless to get outside and have a long gallop.

After breakfast I sent word to Billy, my groom, to saddle Dante and have him ready if the rain should stop. I met briefly with Mrs. Eliott, and then, having nothing else to do, wandered back to my room. I dreaded moments alone, for inevitably my thoughts wandered to John. I was sitting idly by the window watching the rain pound the glass when my fingers chanced to touch the golden key that hung around my neck. For the moment, John's image was gone and my thoughts turned to the two strange letters that were in my letter box. Even before the ball there had not been sufficient time for a letter to reach Peter, since he was leaving Brussels so soon. I decided to read the letters again so I could begin to marshal arguments against Father's rantings when Peter arrived.

I rose slowly and walked over to my writing desk, wondering how I would explain Peter's precipitous arrival. Obviously, I had to devise an excuse to make Peter's visit appear normal to Lawrence. Mechanically I opened the drawer where I had placed my locked letter box. It was not there. Belinda and her continual housekeeping, I thought, frowning. I opened the other drawers, each one more quickly than the one before. The letter box was simply not in my writing desk!

I felt no particular uneasiness as I rang the bell cord for Belinda. I thought with mild exasperation that she must have moved the box to a more appropriate place, in her opinion.

When she appeared, I asked her if she had seen the lacquered letter box. She looked at me blankly for a moment but then brightened.

"Oh, my lady, you mean the pretty painted box in your writing desk?"

"Yes, that is the one," I affirmed. "Did you move it, Belinda? It is no longer in the desk."

"Oh, no, my lady," she exclaimed, much troubled. "The last time I saw it, 'twas right in that drawer." She gestured vigorously to the open desk drawer.

"Well," I replied with more calm than I was now beginning to feel, "we must look for it."

The next half-hour was spent searching the Blue Room. Closets, drawers, boxes, everything was examined thoroughly. The letter box was not to be found.

My uneasiness grew. Not wanting Belinda to see my alarm, I dismissed her, saying lightly, "It is a shame, but of course, not all that important. I am certain that it will be found soon."

She looked unconvinced and said with conviction, "I'll wager my dinner, begging your ladyship's pardon, that it was one of those nasty foreigners who took it!"

"Which nasty foreigners, Belinda?" I inquired, momentarily diverted.

"Those Frenchies, my lady. There was one valet and

two lady's maids—all of 'em Frenchies," she declared, clinching the matter.

"But, Belinda," I said reasonably, "why would anyone—even a nasty foreigner—steal the letter box? It is, after all, of little value compared to other items in this room, which are for more dear and certainly of less conspicuous size."

She still looked unconvinced, but I, on the contrary, was completely certain that no servant, or guest, for that matter, had taken the letter box. I dismissed Belinda. When she left, I began to pace up and down in my room.

There must be a logical explanation to this, I told myself, and I must find it. Quelling my uneasiness, I began to examine the problem calmly. Despite what I had said to Belinda, I began by thinking about our guests. Yes, the majority of them had stayed in the west wing, and anyone could easily have entered the Blue Room unnoticed and taken the box. Accepting this as being true, I frowned, for there was no reason I could see for any guest, or servant, for that matter, to have done such a thing. I realized with certainty that it was not the letter box that would tempt anyone, but rather the letters it contained.

Inevitably my thoughts drifted to the family. Someone had wanted those letters. Even more unnerving was the realization that the person had coldly and intentionally searched my room until he or she had found them. I had been a fool, I thought angrily, ripping the useless gold chain from about my neck.

I could feel a seed of fear planting itself in my mind, growing and pervading my thoughts. But who? was my unsettling question. My husband? Surely not Lawrence! His unflagging kindness and concern for me could not be questioned. Amelia and Thomas. Surely not Amelia. Her initial dislike for me, which I had found perfectly understandable although uncomfortable, had been lessening day by day. And Thomas, smiling Thomas. I could not be certain.

Finally my thoughts turned to John. Just thinking of him brought me renewed anguish. No, I cried to myself, pressing my fists against my temples. it cannot be you, John. I could not bear it!

I suddenly recalled that Mrs. Eliott had been present in the morning room when I had received the letters. Here, at least, was something. But why Mrs. Eliott? Why should she want the letters? There were no answers, only my anxious, endless questions. I desperately wanted to believe that a guest or servant had stolen the box for no other ulterior motive than greed, but I knew, beyond any doubt, that it was someone here in this house, someone close to me. I must accept it and stop being a fool. I had been a fool long enough. I slumped tiredly into a chair next to the fire, trying to work out some sort of plan. I could not remain idly doing nothing.

I did not realize how long I sat by the fire, unmoving, in deep thought, until Belinda tapped on the door, and informed me that Billy had brought Dante to the front drive as I had instructed. Considerably startled, I glanced at the ormolu clock on the mantel. I had been lost in thought for nearly two hours!

"The rain has stopped and the sun is peeping through, my lady," Belinda assured me.

I changed into my riding clothes quickly and hurried downstairs. I hoped that the fresh air and a fast gallop would clear the cobwebs and confusion from my mind. I had to formulate a plan. Also, I wished to be alone, away from the manor and everyone in it.

I came to an abrupt halt at the top of the steps. John was there holding the horses' reins. I stood motionless, flooded with embarrassment and dread, wondering what to do.

John looked up and greeted me casually. "Good morning, Drea."

At the startled look on my face, he added, smiling, "That is what Peter calls you, isn't it?"

Attempting to conceal my agitation, I replied, "Why, yes . . . but how did you know his name for me?"

"You forget, he spoke of you often when we were together."

"Yes, yes, I suppose I had forgotten," I replied uncertainly. I turned away from him, wanting to run back up the stairs and escape.

"Wait a moment, Andrea," he commanded. I turned back and eyed him uncertainly over my shoulder.

He said kindly, "There is no reason for you to go. As a matter of fact, I prescribe a long ride across the fields."

I responded in a small, tight voice, "That is what I intended to do."

"Then let me be your escort," he said gently, holding out his hand toward me.

"But I really would prefer—" I began.

"I promise to be a most comfortable companion," he said, looking at me searchingly. "Also, I regret to say that the poor Billy is quite knocked up with the influenza. Therefore, ma'am, you will have to accept my escort today."

I walked hesitantly down the steps and allowed him to toss me into the saddle.

"Let us be off," he said, after mounting Drago.

At that moment, Dante snorted, pawed the ground, and reared, nearly unseating me.

John's hand shot out, grabbed Dante's bridle, and pulled him down.

My pent-up emotions broke loose and found their release in violent, uncontrolled anger. White with fury, I jerked the reins from John's hand. "Don't you dare do that again," I cried from between clenched teeth.

John's eyes narrowed and he leaned toward me, and said harshly, "I will do whatever is necessary, madam, to prevent you from breaking your willful neck!"

As quickly as my anger had flared, it receded, leaving me weak and shaking. I opened my mouth to say some sort of apology, but he misread my intent, held up his hand, and said dryly, "No, Andrea, acquit me of malicious intent. Let us go, the horses need a good run."

I stared at him, my mouth open, words failing me. After a moment he added in an almost gentle voice, "Come, Drea, let us cry a truce. No more provocations, I promise you!"

"Very well," I managed to mutter in a tremulous voice.

He smiled. The smile filled his eyes, I thought. The now-familiar feeling, like the searing pain of a knife thrust, twisted inside me. I looked quickly away.

If he noticed, he did not let on, but said in a casual voice, "I must call upon a gentleman who lives just west of Shropshire. Have you ridden that way yet?"

I shook my head.

"Good. I know of a shortcut across the fields." He added, eyes twinkling, "I am certain you will approve, for there are many fences for you to take."

We rode side by side down the main drive. Every few steps, Dante tossed his head, reared slightly, and pawed the ground. I leaned over and patted his glossy neck. " 'Tis all right, Dante, we will have a long gallop and you will feel much more the thing."

"What is the matter with Dante?" John asked, reining beside me.

"I suppose he is but restless and fidgety from want of exercise, John."

We turned off the country road that led directly to the village of Shropshire onto an open field that stretched as far as I could see. I pressed my leg hard against Dante's side and loosened my grip on the reins. He needed no more encouragement, and in a few seconds we were racing full tilt across the field. As always when riding, I began to feel exhilarated and free. I took a deep breath, drawing in the fresh, cool air. John rode at my side, keeping an even pace. We continued thus for some time, until in the distance I saw a fence and prepared to jump.

John called to me sharply, "Don't take the jump ahead. It looks as though the storm has blown down a tree just beyond it. It may be dangerous."

I saw the tree and shouted my agreement to John. I began to pull lightly on Dante's reins to slow him and turn him away from the fence. To my utter astonishment, he responded by giving a great snort, plunging his head down, and galloping all the faster straight toward the fence. I tried flattening myself against his neck and grabbing the reins close to his mouth. The trick did not work this time. I could hear John shouting behind me, "Don't be a fool, Andrea. Don't take that fence!"

He misunderstood and thought I was deliberately taking the jump against his advice!

Dante seemed enraged, wild. I knew that he would take the fence, but I did not know why. It was upon us before I could kick my foot free of the stirrup. In that second I pressed myself close against his neck as he sailed over the fence. In midair I could feel him twist under me, trying to throw me from his back. I knew too in that second that he would never be able to maintain his balance. Just before his hooves touched the slippery mud on the other side of the fence, he gave a great cry of anger, tearing the reins from my hands. As he fell toward the fallen tree, I kicked free and jumped, falling on my back on a slight incline. I rolled over and over, clawing at grass, trying to stop my body. A searing pain shot through my head. Before everything went black, I heard Dante's anguished cry of pain as he fell. Then darkness flooded me.

SIX

Slowly I fought my way back to consciousness. I became aware of strong arms encircling me and a voice very far away saying my name. As I opened my eyes, the dark outline of John's face appeared above me. All was blurred except his eyes.

"What very blue eyes you have," I murmured inconsequentially.

I heard a chuckle and felt the arms tighten around me. Again the voice, but this time it was clear.

"Andrea, Andrea, are you all right?" The voice was gentle but insistent.

I managed to open my eyes and gaze somewhat vaguely into his face. "I suppose so," I ventured tentatively.

I tried to sit up, but a searing pain shot through my head and I fell back gladly into the waiting arms. "Oh, my head. It hurts frightfully," I gasped.

"If your head is all that hurts, you are very fortunate, my girl. Try moving your legs."

After a moment of concentrated effort, my legs were convinced to obey. Nothing seemed to be broken. I gingerly reached my hand up and felt the back of my head. When I touched the growing lump, I felt another flash of blinding pain and fell back dizzily. After a moment the pain passed and I suddenly remembered Dante and his anguished cry as he fell.

"John, please . . . Dante," I cried urgently. I tried to struggle up.

"Oh, no, you don't—lie still," he commanded, holding my shoulders.

"John," I repeated, pleading, "please, you must see to Dante. There is something terribly wrong." I ceased trying to move, but gazed up at him with worried eyes.

"I should imagine that there is," he returned shortly. "You forced him to take the fence, and now both of you will suffer the consequences of your folly!"

I was aghast. "No, you don't understand. I tried to stop him but could not. John, please believe me and see to him!"

I thought fleetingly that I was making sense in spite of my aching head and dizziness. I tasted the salt of a tear that had slipped unnoticed down my cheek.

"You didn't cram him?" he demanded harshly.

"Oh, no," I cried. "I couldn't control him. He seemed wild . . . enraged. Please, John, see to him now!" My voice caught in a weak sob.

"Very well, but don't move," he commanded. He stripped off his coat and folded it under my head. I lay back and closed my eyes tightly, hoping to ease the pounding in my head.

At a gentle pat on my arm sometime later, I opened my eyes and looked up into a very worried face.

"How is he?" I whispered. I had never seen John look so grim.

"His right foreleg is badly sprained from the fall, but I think with proper treatment and care that it will heal." He paused for a moment as I let out a sigh of relief. He continued, speaking slowly, his voice measured and deliberate. "I also discovered this under his saddle."

In his hand he held a large, circular band of wire. Attached to the wire were long, sharp barbs, bent downward. The barbs were covered with blood.

My eyes flew to John's face. "I . . . don't understand," I stammered.

He replied evenly, "Someone placed this . . . thing under Dante's saddle. Even your slight weight was enough to bury the barbs deep into his back and side. No wonder he was enraged and wild. The pain must have been excruciating."

At that moment I knew that we were thinking the same thought. Had I not jumped free at the last instant, I would have been crushed under Dante's great body. This was no malicious joke, no apparition to frighten in the middle of the night. Someone had intended to do me serious harm. I felt my face drain of color. John had been looking at me intently, but now I turned my face away. I did not want him to see my fear.

John did not try to dispel my fears by soothing me with reassuring words. When he finally spoke, it was in a calm, matter-of-fact voice. "Do you feel well enough to return to the manor now?"

His manner steadied me. I nodded silently, still unsure that my voice would say what my mind intended. He picked me up in his arms and carried me to his horse.

"I'm afraid that you will have to ride astride."

At that moment I would not have cared had he tied me across the saddle. He lifted me gently up and placed me in the saddle with the admonition "Hold on to the pommel. Steady now," he warned as I began to slip to the side. I gripped the pommel and prayed that I would not fall.

John shrugged quickly into his coat, and I saw him place the vicious barbed circle of wire in his pocket.

When he mounted behind me, I needed no instruction to lean against him, for if I had not, I would have fallen.

"I won't let you fall," he said, encircling me within his arms.

"Dante?" I questioned weakly.

"Don't worry, I'll send Billy for him as soon as we return."

"Thank you, John," I murmured.

He gave a slight chuckle. "Now I know you're sick, if you thank me!"

"Most unfair," I managed to retort, quite unable to bring my wits to bear on a more suitable response.

With each step Drago took, the searing pain shot through my head. Sensing my pain, John stopped our slow progress every few minutes to ease my discomfort.

In a voice that I recognized as my own, I said vaguely, "I fear that I would have been such a coward at Waterloo." Now, why had I said that? I wondered. My mind had not given permission for such a nonsensical thought!

I felt his face come down and brush against my hair. He said in an amused voice, "On the contrary, Drea, you would have routed Boney with your shrewish tongue." After a moment he added in a meditative voice, "I could be brought to feel a great deal of sympathy for the poor man!"

"You're adominable to be taking advantage of my addled wits," I complained weakly.

"I have no doubt that you will have your revenge soon enough, little cat," he returned in a light voice.

Before I could take exception to this, he said quietly, "I think it better that we do not tell anyone about the

. . . cause of your accident. My father, in particular, has been in indifferent health of late, and the concern and anxiety he would feel might prove dangerous."

I was not sure that I saw the logic of this, but I did not have the mental capabilities to decide why. Instead, I asked, "But how then will you explain what happened?"

"A treacherous rabbit hole," he answered promptly.

"What a lowering thought." I sighed.

"Ah, but it was a very deep rabbit hole," he said firmly.

My reply remained unsaid, for a new wave of dizziness flooded me and I once again fell into unconsciousness.

When next I awoke, it was my husband's worried face I saw above me. I heard Thomas say, "It looks as though she's coming around, Father."

I blinked my eyes slowly several times and felt the dizziness begin to recede. I was lying on a sofa in the drawing room, a cool damp cloth on my forehead. Lawrence gave my arm a reassuring squeeze and said gently, "The doctor will be here soon, my dear, just lie still." I heard him say, "No, Amelia, I do not think the smelling salts will be necessary."

Thomas said, "It looks as though John was right, Father. Dante is too strong for her."

"On the contrary, brother," John said hastily, knowing that I would take immediate exception to this, "neither you nor I could have prevented the accident, had we been riding Dante. I assure you . . . it was unavoidable."

"I don't know, John," Lawrence said thoughtfully, "perhaps Thomas is right. In any case, it is quite my fault. You said it was a rabbit hole?"

I could keep quiet no longer. "It was that cursed, wretched rock, Lawrence. If my head had not hit it, all would be well now. Please do not reproach yourself." I was leaning on one elbow, my hair falling over my forehead. The trick, I decided, was to focus on my husband—it made the room stop spinning.

"Very well, my dear," Lawrence replied soothingly. He gently pushed me back against the pillows.

"I think I should like to go to my room," I said shakily, my eyes tightly closed.

My husband carried me upstairs. Belinda was summoned, and soon I was in my nightgown and tucked snugly into bed. Belinda hovered over me, smoothing the bedcloths, changing the damp cloth on my forehead every few minutes, and fluffing my pillows.

"You are acting like a nervous mother hen, Belinda," I whispered.

"My lady, you mustn't talk . . . it'll rattle your head," Belinda scolded.

Much struck by this medical observation, I closed my eyes again and lay very still.

I remember little of Dr. Brice except that his hands were gentle and his voice not too loud. I felt too dizzy and shaky to speak as his fingers probed to see if any bones were broken. The only sound I made was a groan of pain as he touched the tender bump on my head. I heard him say to Lawrence, "I believe, my lord, that her ladyship suffered a slight concussion. I will prepare a draught that will make her sleep."

Someone raised my head, and a vile-tasting liquid was forced between my lips. It reminded me forcibly of the horrible brew Nurse had given me years ago when I had fallen from a tree and broken my arm.

Within a short time the drug took effect and I passed into a deep, dreamless sleep.

I did not again awaken until late the next morning. I opened my eyes very slowly, remembering the pain. But the searing pain did not come, and I felt only a slight, nagging headache. I reached my hand to my head and gingerly felt the bump. It had gone down considerably but was still tender to the touch. Slowly I sat up, pushed my tangled hair from about my face, and looked around me. The room was bathed with the dull, gray light of winter.

I slipped out of bed, pulled off a thick velvet cover, and wrapped it around me. I walked to the window, pulled open the draperies, curled up in a chair, and tucked the cover closely around my body.

In the dull light, the park and home woods looked bleak. There was no sign of life, no movement. Even the strutting peacocks were not to be seen. My eyes strayed to the window casement and the empty holes where the bars had fit. I shuddered involuntarily. Poor Lady Caroline! I jerked away almost instantly from her memory. Lady Caroline did not need my concern or regret. My concern should be with myself, with my own safety and my future in this house.

I began to shake off the final effects of the drug and my own lethargy. The pain of yesterday was gone, and with it the paralyzing fear that had begun in earnest with the missing letters. Grandfather's influence and training had reasserted themselves along with my own streak of common sense.

I looked down at my hands and was surprised to find them formed into fists. My body had shown anger and determination before my mind had recognized it.

What a fool I had been! The Andrea of yesterday now seemed to me like a helpless emotional female. Well, no longer would I be a sentimental fool, allowing confusing emotions and feelings to override my common sense and judgment.

No longer would I desperately try to defend and excuse every member of this household. Now was the time for me to face the truth. The same person who had stolen the letters was the one who had placed the vicious barbed wire under Dante's saddle. Now my father no longer seemed insane. He had warned me to trust no one, and I had been incredulous, totally disbelieving, even in the face of the old woman of that long-ago night. But now I would attend his warning. No one in this house could be immune from suspicion. Not my husband, not Thomas or Amelia, and no, not even John. John. Had it not been he who had brought Dante from the stable? Had it not been he who did not want to tell anyone of the real cause of the accident?

Was there anyone I could trust, anyone who could help me? My thoughts immediately flew to Sophy, but I dismissed the idea of enlisting her aid. Even if Sophy could be trusted, my confidences might place her in danger. No, I could not do that to my dearest friend. I was forced to conclude that there was no one. I was alone, and I had to discover the truth myself.

I considered but a moment my father's advice to flee Devbridge Manor. No, I told myself fiercely, I was not a coward, and now I would be on my guard every minute. I would stay and discover who hated me so much as to deliberately do me harm, or at the very least to try to frighten me into leaving. Filled with determination, I rose and walked quickly to my wardrobe. The first thing I had to do was to go to the stables and see to Dante. Renewed anger flooded me, for my unknown enemy could have killed my horse in the attempt to hurt me. The next thing I would do, I decided, would be to see Mrs. Eliott and confront her about the letters. She was the only person that I knew of who was aware that I had received them. Finally, I would search every room in this house just as coldly and methodically as someone had searched my room to discover the letters. The answer to this mystery had to be somewhere in this house, and I would find it!

I dressed myself in an old muslin gown, ruthlessly pulled a brush through my tangled hair and tied it back with a ribbon. I slipped on a hooded cloak and made my way quietly downstairs.

As I crossed the Old Hall, I heard Brantley's startled voice behind me.

"My lady . . . but surely . . ." He faltered. "After the accident . . ." His voice trailed off in dismay. This was the first time I had seen the staid Brantley lose his impassive dignity.

I turned and said brightly, "Good morning, or should I say good afternoon, Brantley, I assure you that I am restored to excellent health day."

"Yes, my lady," he responded doubtfully.

"I am going to the stables," I continued. "Would you please fetch me some sugar?"

He eyed me dubiously but bowed in assent and withdrew. A short while later, one pocket of my cloak filled with sugar cubes, I walked briskly to the stables. I drew the hood close about my face against the cold, damp air.

Upon entering the stables, I came face to face with a small stable boy, who stood staring at me with an open mouth.

"Where is Dante's stall?" I asked.

He seemed much confused by this and remained speechless, his mouth gaping. I was momentarily diverted, realizing that a female in the stables was not an everyday occurrence. He shifted his weight from one foot to the other, stared at the ground, and tugged fiercely at the shock of bright red hair that fell over his forehead.

I had begun to explain to him why I wanted to see Dante when Billy came walking around the corner. The boy ran to him, exclaiming, "Miss, here, do want Dante, Billy!"

Billy shoved the boy hurriedly aside and rushed over to me.

"Do forgive Jem, my lady, he means no harm. He's a bit befuddled, if you know what I mean." He pointed meaningfully at his head. "Been that way ever since he was a babe," he added.

"It is quite all right, Billy," I said, now understanding why Jem could not comprehend my request.

"Please show me to Dante's stall. I wish to see how he is doing today."

If Billy was surprised at my visit, he made no sign, but turned and motioned me to follow him.

As I entered Dante's stall, he whinned and extended his head to nuzzle my face and shoulder.

"Well, sir," I said as I stroked his forehead, "I fear that you have fared worse than your mistress. All will be well, you will see, my beautiful Dante. You will feel just the thing in no time at all."

I pulled some sugar cubes from my cloak pocket, and he greedily nibbled them off my hand.

"Now, my beauty, let me have a look at your leg." I knelt down and saw that Billy had expertly applied a bran poultice to the injured foreleg.

"How many times a day are you applying the poultice, Billy?" I asked as I turned to look up at him.

"Four times, my lady."

I nodded my approval. Slowly I stood up, careful not to alarm Dante, and examined the deep cuts on his back. Thick ointment covered the wounds.

"And the ointment?" I asked.

"Same as the poultice, my lady."

I gave Dante a final pat, stepped out of the stall, and placed my hand on Billy's arm. "An excellent job, Billy. You are doing everything you can, I know." I sighed. "Now it is just a matter of time."

"Dante will be all right, my lady. I give ye my word,"

Billy reassured. He added, "Master John, he helped me every time to change the poultice. He be very good with animals, Master John."

I ignored the pain that the mention of his name brought me and merely nodded. I refused to willingly express by gratitude to the man who could have been responsible.

When I reentered the manor, I intended to slip quietly to my room to change, for I was hardly fit to be seen in my old dress and with my hair falling loose from the ribbon down my back.

Unfortunately, I met Thomas at the foot of the stairs. He stared at me for a moment in astonishment.

"Good morning, Thomas," I said cheerfully, ignoring his surprise.

"Andrea, whatever are you doing out of bed?" he exclaimed, much agitated.

"I assure you that I am quite well today," I answered smoothly. "You forget, I have enjoyed an excellent afternoon, night, and morning's sleep!" I thought to myself: Are you really so concerned about my health, Thomas?

"If you're really sure that you are all right . . ." he said doubtfully. He then brightened. "Why don't you come to luncheon with John and my father? They are in the morning room."

Thomas had not seemed to notice the state of my apparel.

"Well, I am positively famished," I confessed. I had not eaten since breakfast of the previous day, and the thought of food made my mouth water.

As Thomas opened the door to the morning room, he called out gaily, "look who is here to join us for lunch!"

"Good God . . . Andrea!" John ejaculated, his fork clattering to his plate.

He half-rose, but sat down again as Lawrence hurried

to me. "My dear child, whatever are you doing downstairs?" Noticing my cloak, he added, "And where have you been?"

"I can tell you where she's been, Father," John interposed in an amused voice. Lawrence looked questioningly at me and then at John.

"She's beeen to the stables to see that Dante is receiving the proper care," he said dryly.

"This time you would be correct," I affirmed lightly, as Lawrence helped me remove my cloak and seated me at the table.

"I hope you will excuse my unfashionable attire," I continued, addressing the three gentlemen in general, "but I am very hungry, and Thomas kindly suggested lunch."

"Pray stay seated, my dear," Lawrence directed. "I will serve you."

"Please give me a noble portion of everything, for I am truly famished!"

I did not join the conversation until I had finished a liberal serving of cold chicken, cheese, and warm bread. I was lavishly spreading butter and jam on my third slice of bread when John observed dryly, "A most amazing recovery."

Thomas added, "Of course, Dr. Brice will take the credit. His new reputation should spread all the way to London."

"I only hope that you are not overexerting yourself," Lawrence said, his brow furrowed with worry.

"A relapse would certainly cast poor Brice into agonies and destroy his newfound reputation as well," John said.

"I shall do my best not to disappoint the good doctor." I heard myself laugh and felt my face smile, just as I would have before yesterday, before the accident. Yet today I was inwardly guarded, wary, and somehow detached from all three of them.

I felt John's eyes upon me and turned toward him to see him gazing intently at me. I arched my brows slightly and then casually reached for another slice of bread.

After a moment John asked, "Do you approve of Dante's treatment?"

There was amusement in his voice, but I did not catch it and responded seriously, "I have always found the bran poultice to be very efficacious."

"You know about poultices?" Thomas asked, surprised.

"Of course," I answered shortly, I returned to John. "Billy seems to think that the sprain, with proper treatment, will in time heal. He also said that you were helping him, John. What is your opinion?"

He answered, smiling, "Like you, Dante shows amazing improvement from yesterday."

In answer to my questioning look, he explained, "Yes, I have checked him this morning."

"Well, I for one," said Lawrence gravely, "am relieved on both counts."

"Very true, Father," Thomas said. "But from the way John has described the sprain, Dante cannot be ridden for a fortnight, at the least."

"Quite right, brother, which means that Andrea must have another mount," John said, directing his dark gaze at me.

Lawrence looked at John aghast. "Really, John, Andrea will have no desire to ride so soon after so unnerving an experience!"

"Quite to the contrary, sir," I said swiftly, "I have in no way been unnerved by the . . . accident. I would certainly appreciate another mount until Dante is well."

"She's got pluck to the backbone," Thomas said admiringly.

"Nonsense," I returned shortly. "It is simply a long-established habit and pleasure."

My husband did not answer for a moment. He sat back in his chair, frowning, his arms crossed on his chest. Finally he said heavily, "Very well, my dear, you may ride Trojan."

"But that is your horse, sir," I cried in surprise.

"That is true, and I most willingly will lend him to you for the next sennight."

"But what will you do, Father?" asked Thomas.

Lawrence looked at me ruefully, and after a moment confessed guiltily, "Well, you see, my dear, I really must go to London and am extremely gratified that you are recovered so quickly."

"I see," I replied vaguely, really not seeing at all.

"When must you leave, sir?" I asked.

Both John and Thomas looked at their father expectantly. Obviously they were as surprised as I over this revelation.

Lawrence said, including all of us, "I have postponed this trip several times now." Sensing that his sons would not be content with this explanation, he added, "I must see Barrington in the city about the transfer of some stocks."

John quirked a disbelieving eyebrow, but his father had spoken with finality.

Lawrence, ignoring John, turned and spoke directly to me. "So, if you do not mind, Andrea . . ." His voice was a question.

Doing my expected duty, I answered promptly, "Not at all, sir. When may we expect you to return?"

"By Thursday next, or perhaps sooner, I expect."

I wondered fleetingly why the transfer of stocks was of such importance as to demand his presence at this time, but I remained silent. I did not wish to pursue the subject, for I was also afraid that he might think that I wished to accompany him, which I most assuredly did not. My mind worked furiously. I could begin searching Lawrence's rooms this very night!

Lawrence interpreted my silence in a far different light. He consoled, "It will not be for long, my dear, and I leave you in excellent company." He waved his hand to include both of his sons.

John said lightly, "I promise you, sir, there will be no more rabbit holes."

I looked at him quickly, surprised at his audacity.

"I certainly hope so, else we would run out of horses!" Thomas affirmed, chuckling at his own joke.

We say Lawrence and his valet, Jarrell, off shortly after the luncheon. After making me promise to rest and not to tax myself, Lawrence patted me on the cheek, stepped into his chaise, and was gone. As the chaise bowled down the drive, I felt an undeniable sense of relief. Now I could proceed without fear of arousing Lawrence's suspicions.

I returned to my room to find Belinda much perturbed and indignant at my rise from the sickbed.

"I will wear the yellow-jonquil gown," I commanded, cutting short her protestations.

As she dressed my hair, my mind was busy. I knew that I had to proceed cautiously. No one's suspicions must be aroused. My first problem was Mrs. Eliott. I must in some way break down her defenses so that she could not coldy evade me with her stiff, monosyllabic answers. Words that my grandfather had jokingly used flashed through my mind. "Always strike the enemy at their weakest flank!" I knew Mrs. Eliott's weakness. She invariably became flushed and upset at the mention of Lady Caroline and Judith, and she avoided the child assiduously. The stratagem I decided upon gave me a twinge of guilt, but I shrugged it off. I would invite Judith to dine with the family. This was certainly reasonable in light of the fact that Lawrence was absent. Judith's joining the family for dinner would, of course, involve meeting with Mrs. Eliott to adapt the evening's menu to please a child's taste. Further, I reasoned, it was possible that the missing letters were related to Lady Caroline and Judith. How this could be true, I did not know. But perhaps, just perhaps, I would learn more from Mrs. Eliott and would discover the answers to this mystery!

I went directly downstairs, prepared to carry out my plan. I went to the Ladies' Parlour, pulled on the bell cord, and waited for Mrs. Eliott to appear. I was pretending to study the household accounts when I heard the rustle of her silk skirts. She was wearing her usual severe black gown with but a touch of white lace at the throat.

She gave the slightest of curtsies and said in her flat, toneless voice, "Your ladyship wished to see me?" She evinced no surprise that I could see at my obvious recovery.

"Yes, Mrs. Eliott. Pray be seated."

I indicated a chair opposite my writing desk. She sat down, her back ramrod stiff, her hands folded tightly in her lap. She looked pale, I thought, gazing at her under half-closed lids. Was she already upset about something? So much the better if she were, I thought grimly; it would make my task easier.

"As you know, Mrs. Eliott, his lordship will be absent for a while."

She nodded, her face expressionless.

I pursued. "I have decided to include Judith at the dinner table, beginning with this evening. You will notice," I continued, handing her my revised menu, "that I have added some dishes that she will like."

I noted with satisfaction that her hand trembled as she took the menu from me. Although she kept her head down, in supposed concentration on the menu, her face became flushed with strong emotion. Was it anger? I could not be sure.

For the first time since I had known Mrs. Eliott, I felt that I was in complete control. I sat back in my chair and waited for her to finish reading the menu.

She raised a pale, distraught face.

"Is there anything troubling you, Mrs. Eliott?" I asked without preamble.

Her eyes held mine for a moment. When she finally spoke, her voice was low and tinged with sadness, "No, my lady." She abruptly rose and said hurriedly, "Is there anything else, my lady?" Why should she be sad? I wondered fleetingly.

"Why, yes, there is, Mrs. Eliott. Pray be seated," I commanded, my eyes never leaving her face.

She sat down again, her head bowed.

"You will recall the morning before the ball that I received a letter from my brother. You were there, Mrs. Eliott, and I told you of my brother's letter."

She looked up at me quickly, a puzzled look on her face. "I . . . I do not understand, my lady," she stammered.

She was an excellent actress, I decided. I pursued relentlessly. "There was also a letter from my father, Mrs. Eliott. I placed both of these letters in a lacquered box in my room that same morning and locked it. I discovered after the ball that the letters and indeed my lacquered box were missing."

I leaned quickly forward, grasped her wrist firmly in my hand and said bluntly, "Someone searched my room and stole those letters. You will realize, of course, that the person who did this had to have known about the letters in the first place! What do you know of this?"

My hand tightened on her wrist so that she could not pull away from me.

She heaved a long, deep breath, and I could feel her hand shaking under my grasp.

"Answer me, Mrs. Eliott!" I repeated, my voice insistent.

She raised a pathetically white face to mine. She seemed to be struggling with herself, for her lips moved spasmodically, but no words came out. We sat frozen, like two statues, staring at each other.

She spoke finally in a broken whisper. "You are so young, just as she was young." I knew that she referred to Lady Caroline.

"Yes, Mrs. Eliott?" I urged.

She seemed to catch herself, shut her lips firmly, and looked away from me for a moment. When she spoke again, her voice was calmer, more controlled. "I did not take your letter. I knew only that you had received a letter from your brother."

In that instant I knew that she spoke the truth. "But you know who took them, don't you, Mrs. Eliott?" I pressed, my voice almost gentle.

She did not answer. I continued, my voice rising, "My father's letter was a warning. A warning about someone in this house. Who is that person?"

She tore herself loose of my grasp and jumped to her feet, her breast heaving. She rushed to the door, stopped, and turned to me, panting. Her mouth opened and then closed. She flung out of the room, the door slamming behind her.

I sat frozen, my mind refusing to work, my heart pounding unbearably against my ribs. I had succeeded only too well. Mrs. Eliott's mask had dropped, and I saw her clearly now. She was a terrified woman! What person in this house had the power to make this woman so frightened that she would not speak? I knew now beyond a doubt that it had to do with Lady Caroline, the second Countess of Devbridge. Mrs. Eliott's tortured voice rose in my mind. "She was so young!" She would now have been about the same age as John, I thought, and with that I winced. Had he treated her as he had Lucinda and Lady Elizabeth? I wondered if John had spent all those years in the army of his own accord. I remember Lawrence's hesitancy even to speak of John, as if John's name brought him pain. I rose and walked unsteadily to the window and stood motionless gazing out. You should leave now, today, a small voice inside me repeated over and over. I was on the verge of heeding this advice when I remembered Lawrence's absence. If Lawrence were the person responsible, he could not harm me, at least for the time being. If the person were John, I would have to very careful and wary. I shook my head distractedly. I was affixing blame and guilt, and I had not a shred of proof. In any case, I finally decided, no one could harm me if I kept myself continually surrounded with family and servants. I was not a coward, and I would not leave until I had discovered the person and the reasons behind this deadly game.

The winter afternoon was beginning to darken. If I was going to invite Judith to dine with the family, I must go at once. As I made my way to the schoolroom, I wondered if Sophy was concerned about my accident. I sincerely hoped that she would be glad to see me recovered.

When I entered the schoolroom, Judith stared at me with surprise and exclaimed, jumping up from her chair, "Why, you're supposed to be in bed . . . and very sick!"

Before I could reply, Judith rounded on Sophy and cried indignantly, "You've been roasting me, Gilly. Just look, Andrea isn't ill at all!"

I interposed hastily. "No, dear, Sophy wasn't funning you. Indeed, I have undergone a miraculous recovery, thanks to a vile potion forced down my throat by Dr. Brice."

Sophy crossed quickly to me and clasped my hand warmly in hers. "I am greatly relieved that you did not sustain a severe injury. I have been so worried!"

Judith was still regarding both of us with the profoundest suspicion. She exclaimed with the candor of youth, "I still think it's all a fudge! Imagine *you* having a riding accident."

I ruffled her blond curls and replied in despairing accents, "Alas, it is all too true! My reputation is shattered! And all because of a . . . rabbit hole. A very big rabbit hole," I amended, attempting a justification.

Judith's eyes grew round as saucers as I proceeded to describe the great mythical rabbit hole and its probable occupant.

Sophy began to chuckle, and Judith, after realizing that I was jesting, hunched her shoulder at us, miffed that we had taken gross advantage of her naiveté.

Sophy was in the middle of teasing Judith out of her sullens when a footman entered and informed me that Dr. Brice was waiting in the drawing room.

"He has probably brought some more horrid medicine for you to drink, Andrea," Judith crowed.

"If he has, I shall contrive to pour it in your glass at dinner this evening."

When Judith realized the full meaning of what I had said, she gasped. "What . . . what did you say, Andrea?"

"You, my dear, are to join us for dinner this evening, that is, of course, if Miss Gillbank doesn't mind and if you don't have a previous engagement," I teased, my eyes twinkling at her excitement.

I dismissed the twinge of guilt I felt at not having invited her simply for her own pleasure.

Judith clasped Sophy's hand and cried, "Oh, please, Gilly, say that I might. Please!"

"Of course you shall, love. We will be a merry company."

"Good," I replied, having settled the matter.

As I turned to leave, Sophy said softly, "this is very thoughtful of you, Andrea."

Again I felt a flash of remorse, but quelled it. "Not at all. Sir Lawrence is gone up to London. I thought she would enjoy it."

As I left the schoolroom, I heard Judith ask Sophy excitedly, "Oh, Gilly, please let me wear my hair up!"

"We shall see, poppet, we shall see," I heard Sophy answer fondly.

I entered the drawing room, to be met by a rotund little man wearing a startlingly red waistcoat. The rest of his attire was severe black, denoting his profession.

I extended my hand toward him and said, "How kind of you to come, Dr. Brice. As you can see, I am most fully recovered today."

I had expected the good doctor to be pleased to see me thus restored. I was soon to discover that this was not the case. Indeed, he seemed quite upset at my blooming good health!

"My lady, this is really not the thing! Really not the thing at all," he said in outraged tones, grasping my outstretched hand and leading me to a chair. In a trice, he had sat me down, placed a pillow behind my head, and elevated my feet on a stool.

"Dr. Brice, I do assure you that I am quite fine now," I persisted, trying to rise.

"Oh, no, my lady, nothing could be further from the truth!" he exclaimed, pushing me firmly back into the chair. "You must know, my lady, that you are enjoying but a brief respite before the true effects of your concussion set in," he said portentously.

I stared at him, mouth open.

He began to pace back and forth in front of me, his

hands tugging on the lapels of his red waistcoat. "I really must insist, my lady, that you return to bed at once and stay there for at least a week. I must visit you every day and watch you carefully to be sure that no harmful effects result from your overexertion of today!"

I realized suddenly the reason for his concern. My rapid recovery had cost him a very important patient and a fat fee!

Eyes twinkling, I rose and said gravely, "It is very kind of you to be so involved in your concern, Dr. Brice. I assure you that Sir Lawrence will be most generous since you have effected my cure so quickly. Now, if you will excuse me . . ." I walked resolutely to the bell cord and gave it a tug.

"Really, my lady . . ." he began, then, thinking better of it, bowed and followed the silent Brantley from the room.

There was a distinct twinkle in Brantley's eyes.

I contrived to keep a straight face until the door closed behind them.

I had turned away and was chuckling to myself when I heard John's voice. "I had no idea that our pompous little doctor was so amusing."

I jerked around, to see him standing negligently in the doorway, a slight smile on his lips.

Trying to appear natural, I retorted, "I really feel as though I should be tottering on the brink!" I could feel myself drawing away from him.

"Do you not realize, my dear Andrea, that a lady—and most assuredly a countess—would have the sensibility to suffer at least mild hysterics for a week after such an incident?"

"Oh, how very common of me to recover so quickly," I exclaimed, willing to bandy words until I could get away from him.

I watched him warily as he walked to a sofa and disposed his long limbs gracefully.

He became suddenly serious. "You are feeling just the thing, are you not?" He was looking at me searchingly.

I felt my wariness and calm objectivity crumble under the intensity of his gaze. I turned away quickly to recover my control. When I responded, my voice sounded bright, too bright, and false, even to my own ears. "To be sure, sir, it is but to be forgotten! Your concern is quite unnecessary, I assure you!"

He continued to stare at me, a now thoughtful expression on his face. The silence grew long between us. Finally he said gravely, "I think it wise for us to discuss your accident." As he spoke, he pulled the circle of barbed wire from his pocket. "A most effective device for torture, is it not?"

The sight of the cruel barbs made me blanch. I drew back instinctively. Was he trying to frighten me?

He leaned forward and continued softly, "Really, my dear, we must discuss what is to be done."

I thrust up my chin and said with haughty chill, "I am quite capable of managing my own affairs, John. As I said, your concern is quite unnecessary!"

He stiffened, and his dark eyes bore into mine with blinding intensity. "What the devil!" he exclaimed, rising suddenly and taking a decisive step toward me.

I fairly flew from my chair and to the door. I paused at the threshold and looked back at him fleetingly over my shoulder. He stood rigidly stiff, a bewildered look on his face. He made no movement toward me.

My heart cried out, and I felt tears sting my eyes. I could not leave him thus! I struggled, trying to find something to say that would lessen the intensity of this moment.

It was John who spoke, in a voice of surprising indifference. "I understand that Judith is to join us for dinner this evening."

I managed to reply in a voice of tolerable calm, "Yes, I trust you do not mind."

"Not at all," he said in his lazy, drawling voice of old. After another short pause, he added with deadly sarcasm, "What a very clever stratagem for a new stepmama. It appears that you are taking care of all of us . . . in your own way."

I gasped aloud at his cruel thrust. He stood staring at me, his eyes insolent and hard. My hand flew out as if to ward off his anger. I could feel tears begin to spill onto my cheeks. He must not see me like this! I turned from him quickly and fled from the room.

I paused but a moment outside the door, sobs breaking from my throat. I felt stifled, closed in! I had to get out of this house and away from John and the pain he brought me. Hurriedly I fetched my cloak and let myself quietly out of a side door. I walked quickly across the front lawn toward the home woods.

As I made my way down the path toward the lake, I began to breathe more easily. The cold winter air dried the tears on my cheeks. The silence was absolute, save for the crackling of leaves and twigs under my feet. Even the birds were silent today. I stopped a moment to pull a low branch out of my way. In that brief instant, the total silence was broken by the sound of something moving behind me. I whirled around, nearly losing my balance, my body tensed and ready for flight. I strained my ears, but there was now no sound except my quickened breathing. I stood perfectly still for a moment longer, my eyes frantically searching the woods around me. Had I imagined the noise? I took several quick steps back toward the manor, stopped, and scolded myself. I was becoming a good deal too sensitive, overwrought. I had to get a hold on myself. I turned resolutely and continued my way toward the lake. The noise was probably a rabbit or a pheasant, I reasoned.

I walked briskly through the remainder of the woods to the clearing and stood quietly for a moment gazing out over the lake. Like the winter day, the water was gray, calm, and forbidding. A slight breeze ruffled the thick reeds that grew at the edge of the lake.

I pulled my cloak closely around me and sat down a few feet from the water. As I sat motionless, staring out across the narrow lake, a great wave of loneliness washed over me. This time last year, Peter and I had been at Deerfield Hall with Grandfather preparing for the gay round of winter parties. We had decorated the hall with holly berries and mistletoe and prepared for our guests. We had hunted, danced, ah, so many activities! What a marvelous time it had been. My throat constricted, and tears came to my eyes—tears for what would never again happen, for what was gone forever.

I remained lost in poignant memories, the past vivid in my mind, until I became aware that I was shivering violently from the cold. Dr. Brice's dire predictions rose forcibly to my mind. No, I thought, I mustn't contract an inflammation of the lungs. That pompous little man would be all too delighted to be proved correct, even for the wrong reason!

I rose, shook the grass from my cloak, and turned back toward the woods. From the corner of my eye, I saw something move! Cold anger washed over me, not fear. I yelled furiously, "Who is there? What do you want? You filthy coward, show yourself!"

I heard someone crashing through the woods to my left. I caught only a brief glimpse—it was a man, a burly man dressed in homespuns. He was running away from me! It had to be the man who had followed me here, and he had stood not twenty feet away, watching me! But he had run from me! He had, then, meant me no harm. Who could he be, and why had he followed me? I puzzled. Had Lawrence, in his absence, sent the man to watch me? I could not be certain. I shook my head despairingly, for in fact I could not be certain of the reasons behind anything that had happened to me since my arrival at Devbridge Manor.

Exhausted from all the events of the day, and, I had to admit, from the aftereffects of my accident, I began make my way slowly back to the manor.

When I reached the front lawn, I paused for a moment and looked at Devbridge Manor. It seemed like a great majestic giant framed in the fading gray light of the winter's day. Lights were beginning to appear in the windows. How odd it was that this huge, rambling edifice was my home. I wondered bitterly just how much longer it would remain so.

I stood a moment longer, my eyes scanning the four great wings of the manor. I stopped short, my gaze frozen at the north tower. A light burned brightly, flickered, and then went out. My mind raced. This was impossible! The north wing had been closed off for years! I continued probing the dark tower, when, suddenly, the light flickered on again and became a steady glow.

I broke into a run across the lawn toward the north wing. I had to find out who was there, and why. I chanced to look up again as I ran, and saw, in consternation, that the light had disappeared and the tower was plunged into darkness. I stopped, panting, unsure what to do. Night was rapidly descending. I realized that I would have great difficulty finding my way, and if I were late for dinner, I might arouse someone's suspicions. I hunched my shoulders in frustration. I had to go change for dinner now, but tonight, after I had searched my husband's rooms, I would go to the north tower.

I glanced one last time at the north tower, now bathed in darkness, and walked resolutely into the house.

SEVEN

In five years, Judith would be the toast of London, of that I was certain. Already she was an uncommonly pretty girl; she would become a lovely woman. Sophy had dressed her with her usual quiet good taste and had threaded a blue ribbon through Judith's loose fair curls. I wondered how Sophy had talked Judith out of wearing her hair up.

Amelia's initial disbelief at spending an evening with a schoolgirl dissipated quickly. Indeed, she rose admirably to the occasion, even going so far as to express a desire to see Judith's needlework.

Judith was at first shy, blushing and stammering when one of us addressed her. As the meal progressed, however, she became more confident and animated, delighting in her first dinner party. When, at the close of the dinner, James, a footman, set before her a rich concoction of whipped cream and nuts atop an apple tart, she went into such raptures that even Amelia laughed aloud in friendly amusement.

The gentlemen did not linger long over their port and soon joined us in the drawing room. John most gallantly suggested a game of lottery tickets. This drew a most unladylike cry of delight from Judith.

I flashed him a quick look of gratitude, only to be repelled by a cold, hard glance. I took a deep breath and tried to tell myself that I did not care what he thought of me.

Though none of us had played at lottery tickets for years, Judith's excitement and total absorption in the game had a powerful effect. I threw myself into the game, willing myself to forget for the moment what I had to do this night. John competed fiercely to win fish (which he managed to adroitly lose to Judith), and Amelia was heard to utter several cries of delight or dismay, depending upon her luck at the moment. Thomas, I decided, smiling at him, would be perfectly happy doing any activity one suggested.

When Brantley entered bearing the tea tray, I was quite surprised at how quickly the time had passed. Shortly after tea, Judith, weary but flushed with pleasure, bid us a charming good night and accompanied Sophy upstairs. I excused myself but a short time later, my eyes avoiding John as I said my good nights.

The gaiety of the evening faded quickly as I slowly mounted the stairs. I began to focus my thoughts in earnest toward what I had to do. I would have to appear natural around Belinda, allow her to prepare me for bed, and dismiss her in my usual manner. Since the evening was not well enough advanced, I would simply have to stay in my room and wait. How I wished that Peter were here. He would help me find the key to this maze!

Belinda awaited me in the Blue Room. As she helped me to undress, she maintained a steady flow of light chatter, punctuated with scolds whenever she looked upon my pale, tired face.

Finally I broke in, saying, "Belinda, please stop reading me lectures! You make me feel as though I should be curling up my toes and awaiting to be carted off!"

As an afterthought, I added with a chuckle, "You and Dr. Brice would suit admirably. You share the same morbid opinions and the same melancholy predictions."

Scandalized, Belinda clamped her lips tightly shut—a sure indication that I had offended her sensibilities. Normally I would have instantly regretted my sharpness and teased her out of her sulks. But tonight I could not be concerned. My mind was fully occupied with my plans.

I dismissed Belinda, locked the door, walked over to the dying fire, and curled up in a chair. I glanced up the clock, and realized that I had to wait at least another hour to be sure that the family and all the servants would be in bed. The room was becoming chilly, so I rose and walked over to my bed. At least I could be warm while I waited. I pulled back the covers. Lying on the white sheet was a gleaming knife! I gasped and recoiled in shock, stepping back instinctively. The vivid memory of that night came rushing back. The old woman walking slowly toward the bed, the glittering, curved knife she held high above her head, ready to descend and strike. It was the same knife; of that I was certain! Gingerly I grasped the delicately carved gold-and-silver handle and brought it close to the candlelight for a closer inspection. There was some sort of inscription on the handle, but I could not make it out. The blade was curved like a scimitar and was deathly sharp to the touch. I sat staring a long moment at this deadly instrument. I began to tremble violently as I stared at the knife, living and reliving that terrifying night. My hand went instinctively to my breast, and I could almost feel the cold, sharp blade touch my skin. I felt drained and more afraid than I had ever been. It was obvious that I had more than one enemy in this house. My mind flew back to the man who had followed me to the lake. Was he waiting outside my door at this very moment? Where was the old woman? Was everyone in this house against me? My carefully laid plan to search my husband's rooms and the north tower seemed, at this moment, absurd. It now seemed foolhardy for me to wander around the manor in the dead of night, and much too dangerous! I would have to wait until the morning, when I could at least see if anyone followed me or was watching me.

I picked up the knife and laid it carefully in a drawer in the night table. It was another clue, another piece to this puzzle.

I blew out my candle and burrowed under the covers, feeling more alone than I had ever felt in my life.

I dreamed that night that I was standing below the north tower watching a candle flicker eerily in the window. John appeared, leaned out of the window, and beckoned to me. As he held out his hand to me, he began to laugh. I was running, running toward him, my arms flung wide. As I neared the window, John suddenly lifted his arm, and in his hand he held the knife. He continued to laugh, arcing the knife up in preparation for a deadly strike. His strong white teeth gleamed. My scream died on my lips as I woke with a start, clutching at the neck of my nightgown. I was wet with perspiration, and tendrils of hair clung to my damp forehead. I pushed my hair back from my face and gave a nervous laugh. My own voice reassured me, for I knew that I was awake. It had only been a horrible dream.

The remainder of the night, I tossed and turned, and what little sleep I had was fitful.

I received only a curt nod in response to my "good

morning." John lowered his head immediately and continued to eat his breakfast. We were alone in the breakfast room.

"Where is Thomas?" I wondered aloud.

John looked up and replied with some intolerance, "Thomas fancied he was coming down with a cold. I assume he is still in bed, quacking himself."

"Perhaps it is wise for him to be cautious," I replied in a noncommittal voice.

There was silence between us until John, finished with his breakfast, pushed back his chair, rose, and strode toward the door. As he passed my chair, he paused and looked down at me for a moment. He asked in an abrupt voice, "Do you wish anything from the village?"

"No, thank you, John. But there is something I would like to show you now, if you have time."

He shrugged. "What is it?"

I took the plunge. My hand shook slightly as I pulled the knife from my pocket. I had carefully wrapped it in one of my handkerchiefs. I heard John's sharp intake of breath as the glittering knife emerged from the cloth.

"Where the devil did you get that knife?" he demanded in a hard voice. He took the knife from my hand and examined it closely.

"Then you recognize it?" I asked, my voice barely above a whisper.

"Of course . . . it's mine," he declared flatly. "It is from my Spanish collection. This particular knife is Moorish, and quite old."

He looked up at me, frowned, and repeated his question. "Where did you get it, Andrea?"

"It was in my bed last night," I answered dully.

"Perhaps you would explain more fully, so that I may understand you," he said almost savagely.

I wondered why he was so angry. After all, what had I done?

"If you wish it," I replied tonelessly. I looked up into his wrathful face and felt the color drain from my own.

"Well, Andrea?" he pressed, his lips curled.

I began slowly. "You recall my nightmare visitor when I first arrived here?"

John nodded, his eyes narrowing.

"The old woman in that nightmare was carrying this knife. I recognized it immediately when I found it in my bed last night."

"You are certain?" His voice was more a statement than a question.

I nodded mutely.

John walked to the long windows and stood staring out silently. Still with his back to me, he said evenly, "It was about a month ago that Ferguson noticed that the knife was missing from the collection. He is not the most sterling of housekeepers."

He turned and crossed toward me. I rose quickly from my chair. "The knife could have been taken perhaps even a . . . month or two before."

"Yes, yes, of course, that is possible." I sighed wearily. I turned away from him. I wanted to leave this room, this house, to be alone. My world was crumbling and turning to ashes. My mouth felt dry, and my eyes stung from unshed tears. Of course the knife had been stolen from his collection. What else could he say? I felt tired, very tired.

In a swift movement John whirled me around and grasped my wrists in his hands. "Look at me," he commanded.

I raised my head slowly and met his intense gaze unflinchingly.

"Do you believe that I am responsible for all that has happened to you since you came here?" he demanded savagely.

I said nothing, for I could not be certain, and I would

not lie. I wondered if he could see the naked pain in my eyes.

He flung me violently away from him. I clutched at the table to keep from falling. In a voice tense with suppressed emotion he cried, "God knows I never wanted you here! The moment I saw you, I knew that I could not remain, seeing you as my father's wife!" His voice was suspended for a moment. He exploded furiously, "For you to believe that I . . . that I would ever want to harm you, that I would ever want to cause you pain . . ."

He stared at me, incredulous. I looked away quickly for tears were filling my eyes. I was gripping the table edge so tightly that my fingers were white and almost numb from the pressure I was exerting.

The only discernible sound in the room was John's heavy breathing. I stood rigid, my back to him, forcing myself not to turn and run to him.

The next sound I heard was his quick, firm stride to the door. He flung it open and was gone. The door banged shut with such force that the glasses trembled on the table. I stayed as I was, bending over the table, clutching the side. It was not that I needed the table to support me from falling. The table represented something real, something that I could be certain of, something solid and firm under my grip. Oh, God! I had made such a mull of my life since Grandfather died!

"Do you wish the fire set, my lady?"

"No, thank you, Brantley. I shall be here only a short time. It is not worth the bother."

"Very good, my lady."

"Oh, Brantley, would you please see that I am not disturbed."

"Yes, my lady." Brantley bowed and closed the library doors quietly behind him. If he was curious as to why I should choose to come to this dark, cold room, he did not betray the fact.

I shivered as I stood looking at the rich, dark furnishings. Three walls were covered with bookcases filled with books. There was a globe in one corner, and several escritoires. Several large leather sofas and chairs were arranged around the fireplace. The heavy brocade curtains closed out the light, making the room dim and chill. Where should I begin looking? I wondered. And for what?

I walked to the large, exquisitely carved desk that stood at the far end of the library. My feet made no sound on the thick carpet.

The top of the desk was bare save for a few books. I thumbed through these quickly. I pulled the top drawer open, relieved that it wasn't locked. I carefully began sorting through the neatly stacked papers. How like Lawrence, I though. So well ordered. All the papers seemed to concern estate business and tradesmen's accounts. I sorted through each of the other drawers, finding that they too contained the same kinds of papers and account ledgers. I closed the bottom drawer and sank down into the ornately carved desk chair. I had found nothing, not the slightest clue, nothing in the least suspicious. I was unsure whether I felt relief or disappointment.

I opened the library door slowly and peered out. There was no one in sight. I walked quickly up the stairs, stopped at the landing, and looked around me. The hallways were empty. I quickly turned and hurried in the direction of my husband's rooms. My hand trembled as I reached for the doorknob. How grateful I was that Jarrell had accompanied his master. At least I did not have to worry about him surprising me in Lawrence's rooms!

I opened the door, slipped in quickly, and closed it

softly behind me. I gasped in surprise as I looked about me. The room was huge, but stark and austere in its furnishings. There was no carpet on the floor, and what pieces of furniture there were seemed to emphasize the bareness of the room. It was a severe, cold, and forbidding place. I walked slowly about the room, feeling the chill atmosphere penetrate my gown. This room reflected a man of sober, almost monkish character. I realized how little I knew of the man, for to me he had always appeared to be elegant and polished, a man who enjoyed the luxuries of life. A noise sounded behind me. I whirled around, my pulses racing, only to feel foolish, for my full sleeve had knocked over a small enamel snuffbox from a small table. I sucked in my breath. I had to cease thinking about the strangeness of this room and the man who occupied it and begin my search. I walked rapidly to a dressing table and opened the drawers. There were only brushes, combs, nail files, and shaving tools. I straightened and walked to the night table beside the daised bed. There were no drawers. Only chairs and sofas remained. I stood in the middle of the room, looking about me, when I saw another door. It led into the adjoining dressing room. This room contained only armoires. I searched through these quickly, embarrassed at going through my husband's personal articles. There seemed to be nowhere else to search, I thought despairingly. My eyes traveled over the ornately carved wood paneling that covered three walls of the dressing room. It seemed odd to me that such exquisite craftsmanship was relegated to a dressing room.

I was beginning to think that my only hope now lay in finding a clue in the north tower, when I chanced to see a slight indentation in one of the panels. Excitement welled up in me as I quickly walked to the panel and began to explore the recessed area. I ran my fingers over the wood, probing, searching. To my surprise, my fingers touched a small curved spring, and a low, narrow door creaked open. I stood stock-still for a moment, my stomach jumping uncomfortably. I peered uncertainly through the aperture and then tiptoed in. The room was tiny and airless, for there was but one small window, and it was closed. One small writing desk and a hard wooden chair stood in the center of the room. This was indeed a private place, a place where I should not be. I wondered what Lawrence was like when he was in this room. Trembling, I walked to the desk and sat down in the chair. There were three small drawers in the desk, and I found myself hesitating for a moment, realizing that this was the ultimate invasion of my husband's belongings. I resolutely opened the top drawer. It was filled with neat stacks of letters, each stack tied separately. All the letters seemed to be personal correspondence, many of them yellowing with age. I picked up each stack and thumbed quickly through them. There were letters from Lady Pontefract, Lord Holliston, Lady Smithson-Blake—all people whose names I had heard, but had never known. They were names my grandfather would mention, prominent figures of my grandfather's time—and of my husband's.

It was at that moment, sitting in that austere, narrow room, holding letters of love, of intrigue, of politics, that I consciously admitted to myself for the first time what I had done. Those fading, yellowing letters were symbols of the mistake I had made. I had married a man who belonged to the century before—to the French Revolution, to the rise of Napoleon, to the great naval victories of Lord Nelson. I adored that world, for it held limitless fascination, but it was not real; it was not a part of my world.

Peter had been right. I had tried to escape my time, my world, by marrying a man who was too old to touch my heart, or my fears. I had sought a continuance of the freedom and protection my grandfather had provided me. Freedom and protection! These thoughts brought a twisted smile to my lips. But I really could not discover the irony in my situation, only despair at my own folly.

I looked down at my hands. I had crumpled the edges of some of the letters from gripping them so tightly. Smoothing them out carefully, I placed them neatly back and closed the drawer.

The second drawer contained only writing materials and elegant stationery. I tugged at the third drawer, only to realize a moment later that it was locked. Perhaps it held an answer! I pulled a pin from my hair, twisted it slightly, inserted it carefully into the small lock, and moved it back and forth. Nothing happened. I moved it more vigorously. The next instant the lock sprang loose and the drawer slid open.

The drawer was empty save for one envelope. It was addressed to his lordship, the Earl of Devbridge, postmarked London. I pulled out the enclosed sheet of paper and smoothed it out on the desktop. It read:

My Lord:

8 December, 1818

Edward Jameson has just arrived in London. I await your instructions.

Your obedient servant,
Grafton

My head was in a whirl! My father was in London? What instructions? Why would Sir Lawrence give "instructions" about my father to this man named Grafton? I read and reread the few lines, trying to make some sense out of them. It was no use. I had so urgently sought to find some clue, to discover the answer to this deadly game I was trapped in. Now the clue I had searched for was in my hand, and still I did not understand. The date! It was but three days before my riding accident! I put the letter down and pressed my fingers against my throbbing temples. Now I realized that my father's warning was against Sir Lawrence. That was why he was so shocked and dismayed at my marriage! But what had my father to do with all this? I still did not know the reasons.

I had now to accept the truth that Sir Lawrence, my husband, was the person who wanted to kill me, or at least to harm me. But why, my mind cried out, why did he marry me? What had I done to deserve his hate?

I stared about me. I had been here all too long. Someone might come and discover me! I quickly returned the letter to its envelope and replaced it in the drawer. I closed the drawer and inserted the hairpin. Frantically I moved the pin back and forth until, finally, mercifully, the lock clicked back into place.

I secured the small, hidden door back into place, and fairly raced through the dressing room to the main bedroom. I shivered as I crossed quickly across the cold wooden floor to the door. I again peered anxiously up and down the hall, slipped out of the room, and pulled the door quietly closed behind me.

I stopped, panting for breath at the top of the landing, to marshal my thoughts. Of a certainty, Lawrence was responsible for what was happening to me. But who was the old woman? It could not have been Lawrence, for he had joined John and me much too quickly. Who had left the knife—John's knife—in my bed? A deep sense of relief flooded over me at the thought of John. It seemed totally fantastic that he could be in league with his father. No, there was too much dissension and distrust between them. My mind flew to the candlelight I had seen in the north tower the previous evening. Who had been there? Was it the man who had followed me to the lake?

Well, I decided firmly, there was but one way to find out—I must go now to the north tower.

I saw no one as I opened the heavy oak door that divided the north wing from the rest of the manor. The long corridor was not carpeted, and the only sound to be heard was the clicking of my heels on the flagstone. I did not enter any of the chambers, but hurried directly to the small tower door at the end of the long passage. The smell of dust and decay filled my nostrils, and the air was damp and chill. The tower door was heavy, and it took all my strength to pull it open. It finally gave a protesting creak, and I was faced with narrow, uneven stairs that bent around out of view. As I slowly mounted the stairs, dust and cobwebs clutched at my skirt. It took all of my courage to climb those stairs, for I now felt fear of something unknown. This tower had seen two violent deaths. I shivered, thinking of the poor governess, murdered so long ago by the jealous wife. The poor Lady Caroline. She had hurled herself in her madness from the turret room!

My fear grew as I neared the top of the circular stairs. I forced myself to go on. When I came around the last bend, I was faced with another, smaller door. For a moment my hand refused to go to the handle. Finally I clutched the heavy iron handle and shoved with all my might. The door creaked open under my insistent weight, and I found myself standing in a small circular room. It was made all of stone, stone that had become damp and chill through the years. There were four long, narrow windows. Each, I thought, wincing, was quite wide enough for a person or for a body to go through, or to be shoved through. The only piece of furniture was a large wooden chest in the middle of the room.

I knelt down in front of it and pulled at the latch. It opened easily. I do not know what I expected to find, but I was surprised to discover that the chest contained gowns. I carefully lifted the top gown out and laid it on the stone floor beside me. It was an old, elegant gown of heavy brocade, from long ago. The waist was tightly fitted and the skirts full over panniers. It was a dress my grandmother would have worn, or, I thought bleakly, Lawrence's first wife.

There were several other gowns in the chest, all of the same style and era. I laid each of them gently on the floor. I lifted out the last dress, when I reeled back on my heels, a scream dying on my lips. There, staring up at me, were the eyeless holes of a hideous mask! It was the face of the old woman! I extended my unwilling hand and picked up the mask to examine it more closely. It was very lifelike, so real, in fact, that gooseflesh rose on my arms at the touch of it. Under it was a wig of long tangled white hair and a long, flowing white robe. Now, I thought grimly, I had the proof that the old woman had not been a ghost or an invention of my own imagination. I sat back on my heels to think. Finally, one mystery was solved. Whoever had placed John's knife in my bed had been in the tower room the previous evening to fetch it. That person had lit the candle I had seen from the front lawn. That person had also played the part of the old woman. Still, my discovery had brought me no closer to identifying the person.

I carefully placed all the articles back into the chest, closed the lid, rose, and hurried from the tower room. I made my way back down the winding stairs. As I closed the tower door behind me, I saw with dismay that my gown was covered with dirt and cobwebs. I brushed it off as best I could, fearing that someone would see me before I could reach my room. To my great misfortune, a footman passed me as I crossed the upper landing. He bowed and stood aside, his face alight with curiosity.

I quickly entered my room, and locked the door behind me. The Blue Room had never seemed so welcome.

For the moment, at least, I felt safe, safe from my husband and from my other enemy. I sank wearily into a winged chair close to the fire and basked in its warmth. I fanned my hands toward the blaze and felt the gentle heat flow into my body. I had learned much today, perhaps more than I had bargained for. Whatever was I to do now? My thoughts flew to John, and I wondered if I could now ask him to help me. Would he help me against his own father? Would he even believe me if I told him what I had found? I remembered his violent anger of that morning. Perhaps he did not care now; perhaps he despised me. A tear rolled down my cheek, and I brushed it away angrily. There seemed to be no one I could turn to. I thought of Peter. But, no, I could not expect him until Christmas, nearly two weeks away. I realized glumly that I did not even know where he was. I could not even contact him.

The flames began to dance in front of my eyes, and my head began to feel heavy. My fitful night's sleep combined with this day's discoveries had left me feeling exhausted. I leaned my head back against the soft cushions of the chair, and soon I fell into a deep sleep.

I was awakened by an insistent knock on the door. I rubbed the sleep from my eyes and pushed back my hair, trying to chase away the drowsiness.

"My lady. My lady." Belinda's voice accompanied the insistent knock.

"Just a moment, Belinda," I called, rising.

"My lady, your gown!" she exclaimed when I had let her in.

"I have been exploring, Belinda, and you must know that one cannot enjoy such an experience without becoming perfectly filthy!" My voice sounded light and unconcerned.

"I'll have a nice hot bath fetched for you, my lady." She eyed me once again with obvious distaste and added,

"But first we must get you out of this . . . this garment!"

"Why, Belinda, this is—was—once a lovely dress," I teased.

"Well, 'tis only fit for the poor now, my lady." She clucked with disapproval and shook her head. She continued to scold as she undressed me. This evening I found her concern for me reassuring and comforting. In this entire house, my personal maid was the only one I really trusted. I turned impulsively and gave her a quick hug. "You're a treasure, Belinda!"

"My . . . my lady," she stammered, "you . . . are too kind and good."

"Stuff and nonsense," I replied heartily.

This more normal comment brought back her brisk manner, and she said firmly, "Now, my lady you just sit right down here in front of the fire and keep your dressing gown wrapped snug. I'll have your bath fetched up right away." She fussed over the arrangement of the dressing gown and then hurried to the door.

"Oh, Belinda," I called after her, "please inform Brantley that I will not be dining downstairs this evening. I am feeling very tired. A tray in my room will be fine."

"Yes, my lady." Her tone implied that her predictions about my premature rise from the sickbed had been proven correct.

A short time later I sank into the warm, scented water of my bath, letting it reach a level right below my chin. My sleep had refreshed me, and I no longer felt exhausted. I felt alert, calm, and poised for action.

Sir Lawrence would be returning within the next four or five days, and by that time I had to decide what action I would take, and, if need be, carry it out before his return.

My thoughts were interrupted by a knock at the door. Belinda had placed screens around the copper tub, so I could not see who it was. I made out Brantley's voice but could not understand what he was saying to Belinda.

"What is it, Belinda?" I asked impatiently, as she came around the screens.

"It's his lordship, my lady. He had just arrived but a short time ago and hopes you will be refreshed enough to join the family for dinner."

I jumped to my feet, my heart pounding, water spilling over onto the carpet. "When did his lordship arrive?" I cried sharply.

"My lady!" Belinda did not answer my question until she had modestly wrapped me in a large soft towel.

"When, Belinda, when?" I again demanded, a definite edge to my voice.

She looked at me with some surprise and answered in a concerned voice, "About an hour ago, according to Brantley, my lady."

I heaved a rather shaky sigh of relief. Thank God he had not arrived earlier and found me searching his room!

"Do you wish to dine downstairs now, my lady?" she asked, curiosity and concern blending in her voice.

"Yes, yes. No . . . oh, I suppose so," I answered distractedly.

Belinda must have thought that she was dressing a doll or a puppet, so mechanically did my body respond to her proddings and lacings. But my mind was working at a furious pace. I had to dissimulate, just as I had done with Belinda. I had to hide what I was feeling. My husband must not realize what I knew. He must not sense fear or suspicion from me. I had to play a role that I had never played before, and perhaps my life depended on my skill.

I turned toward the mirror. A pale, worried face stared back at me. With the greatest deliberation I smoothed away the frantic look and replaced it with a bright smile. I became aware of how elegantly Belinda had dressed me. She had selected a gown of dark green velvet with a high waist and long fitted sleeves. The neckline was low and edged with a row of delicate gold lace.

"Good God, Belinda," I exclaimed, realizing that I had not responded when she asked which gown I wanted to wear. "I am not being presented to the regent this evening!"

"Well, your ladyship seemed quite excited when you learned of his lordship's arrival," she answered defensively.

So Belinda had mistaken my shock and fear for a bride's excitement! Perhaps I was more adept at dissimulation than I knew. I gave her a bright smile and murmured in a light voice, "Quite right, Belinda. You were quite right!"

The bright smile remained on my face as Brantley held open the door for me to pass through into the drawing room. My husband was leaning against the mantel, a glass of sherry in his hand, talking to Sophy. She was seated gracefully in a winged chair next to him. Amelia sat opposite, twirling her glass between long graceful fingers, looking somewhat distracted. To my dismay, neither John nor Thomas was present.

"What a wonderful surprise, sir!" I exclaimed, obvious pleasure and excitement in my voice.

I stretched my hands toward him as he quickly deposited his sherry glass on a table and strode over to me. He grasped my hands in a strong grip and said provocatively, "Ah, my dear, what man would not hurry home with such a beautiful and charming lady awaiting him!"

"Sir, you are in unprincipled flatterer, albeit an accomplished one," I replied, laughing.

He leaned over and brushed his lips lightly against my cheek. It took all my resolution not to recoil from his touch. As he straightened, I gazed directly up into his face. Either he had changed or this was the first time I noticed that above his smile his eyes were a cold gray, like steel. His eyes held mine, as though he were trying to probe into my mind. I gave a nervous laugh, tore my gaze from his, and bid good evening to Sophy and Amelia.

"How is Thomas this evening?" I inquired of Amelia as I seated myself beside her.

She waved a languid hand and sighed wearily. "Poor dear, he is really quite knocked up."

If I did not know Amelia's indolent nature so well, I would have supposed that she had been in constant attendance over the sickbed.

"I do hope he will be on the mend soon," Sophy said in her gentle voice.

Amelia acknowledged this kind sentiment with another weary nod, and then we fell silent. Normally the absence of conversation was diverting, for it meant that no petty squabbles were afoot. But tonight, after a moment of silence, my hands were damp with perspiration and my fingers were clutching the folds of my gown. I had to do something, say something, I thought frantically, or else Lawrence will know for certain that something is amiss.

"Lawrence," I cried gaily, flashing him what I hoped was my most animated smile, "you have not yet told us about your trip. We were not expecting you for another four or five days!"

"My dear," he responded, " I would never recount such boring matters to such charming company."

"Come, Lawrence," I cajoled, "you scarce had time to reach London. You must tell us what you were about."

"Very well, my dear, if you must know." It was as if he were giving in to a coaxing child. "It so happened that there was a mix-up in communications with my man of business in London. As chance would have it, I met him on the road on his way to Devbridge Manor! And so," he concluded, "we mutually agreed to conduct our business at the George Inn in Stowbridge."

He is lying, I thought. Why had he really come back so soon? Did his trip have something to do with me?

Again silence reigned. I glanced over at Sophy. She looked withdrawn this evening, as though she were far away from us. Decidedly, polite conversation was the farthest thing from her mind. Where in heaven's name was Brantley? Would dinner never be announced?

Lawrence strolled back to the fire and asked of no one in particular, "John will not be gracing us with his presence this evening?"

Amelia shrugged a white shoulder and said somewhat petulantly, "He *would* go dine with the Applecrofts this evening!" She added, grinning, "I understand that Lady Applecroft is absent—attending an ailing sister, I believe."

A lump formed in my throat and threatened to choke me. I swallowed convulsively. Stop it, my girl, I commanded myself, it is no time to be the jealous woman.

Amelia continued in a mocking voice, "It would serve him right if Lady Applecroft would return in the middle of the first course!" Her face lighted up as she contemplated the possible outcome of such a marvelous scene.

Lawrence cocked an eyebrow at Amelia and asked in an amused voice, "Is the fair Lucinda not desirable enough to attach John, even though her matchmaking mama were present?"

Amelia refused to be drawn. "That simpering little flirt! John is but amusing himself, my dear sir. But recall the lovely Lady Elizabeth. Why, when she was here, he scarce noticed anyone else." She lightly tapped her father-in-law's arm with her fan, a laughing challenge in her eyes.

Lawrence looked down at her lovely face and said reflectively, "Perhaps you are right, my dear. But remember that Lady Elizabeth is a married woman. So he must look elsewhere. Do not forget that John must marry and set up his nursery!"

"Very true, sir," Amelia retorted quickly, "but regardless, he would never allow marriage to interfere with his pleasures!"

Amelia turned toward me, I suppose for confirmation of her opinion. To my dismay, she exclaimed, "Why, Andrea, you are so pale! My dear, are you feeling quite the thing? I do hope you have not caught Thomas' cold. Oh, dear, I did hope that he would not be contagious!"

How grateful I was to Amelia for explaining my sudden pallor. I summoned a smile to my lips and said to the company in general, "Amelia is probably right. I have not been feeling quite the thing today."

Lawrence was looking at me steadily, his eyes boring into mine. His voice, however, was all gentle concern. "I hope you have not been trotting too hard, my dear, since I have been away."

Did he know something? No, it was impossible. I gave a brittle laugh and said lightly, "Oh, no, sir, except, of course, for last night." I then regaled him with an account of our evening with Judith.

By the time I had finished, Brantley appeared and announced dinner. I laid my hand on Lawrence's proffered arm in relief, and we walked silently to the dining room.

Dinner seemed interminable. Although I had no appetite, I forced myself to take a bite or two from each dish so that no one would think something amiss. My mind was in a whirl. One moment I was trying to think of the best way to outwit my husband, and the next I was feeling jealousy about John. A great bitterness flowed over me as I thought about Amelia's words before dinner. First Lucinda and then Lady Elizabeth! Not even marriage would change him! I bit my lip and told myself that to love John was madness, for he was just like my father—a rake and an unconscionable womanizer, incapable of genuine feeling, incapable of love.

When dinner was finally concluded, the four of us returned to the drawing room. To my dismay, Sophy excused herself, pleading a headache, and Amelia repaired to the sickroom. I stood facing my husband.

"It appears, my dear, that we are to amuse ourselves this evening. Shall we pass the time with a game of chess?"

"An excellent suggestion, sir," I responded with tolerable calm.

I fetched the chess pieces from the buhl cabinet as Lawrence arranged the chess table in front of the fire. As he held my chair for me, he said softly, "You seem very wan tonight, Andrea. I insist that you play the white pieces. They match your so-interesting pallor."

My eyes flew to his face, but I could read no signs of irony or maliciousness written there.

"Perhaps, I have indeed been trotting too hard after my accident," I agreed. "But be forewarned, sir, I fully intend to vanquish your black forces!" I added. I smiled stiffly.

My first moves were mechanical, moves that I knew and could make without thought. My King pawn to the fourth square, my Knights to their Bishop posts. Several moves later as I reached my hand out in an automatic move to castle my King, I chanced to look at my husband's face. Blatant condescension was clearly written there, and a marked sneer played about his lips.

In that second, I raged inwardly, forgetting my calm-and-steady stratagem. Did he really think me such a witless, stupid woman? Condescension indeed! I would show him! I flashed him an arch, coquettish smile that denoted, I prayed, a total lack of comprehension of what I had read on his face. I quickly lowered my head and began furiously to study the arrangement of the chess pieces. I soon discovered that if I had castled my King, my Queen would have been lost but a move later under check by his Knight. It was a deceptively simple trap, one that would not pass unnoticed to a chess player of any merit. No wonder the patronizing look—I was not even a worthy adversary in a game of chess! I ignored the small voice inside me that warned of the mistake I was making. I would show him that I was indeed an opponent to be reckoned with! I could not doubt that my husband would wonder at my intense concentration and feeling. No matter! At that moment, the game of chess symbolized my own victory or defeat in this house.

My intensity did not long escape my husband, and soon his concentration equaled my own. What he was thinking about the obvious change in me, I could not even guess, for the look of condescension and the sneer were now replaced by a very even, impassive expression.

I searched and struggled to find the best moves. Time and again I was rebuffed, but my determination only strengthened.

There was no sound in the room. At one point, Brantley entered with the tea tray, and seeing us totally engrossed in the game, departed as silently as he had entered, pausing only long enough to build up the fire.

At last I saw my way! I moved my Knight to a crucial square without threat from the black pieces. Within a few moves my Queen and her Bishop were bearing down upon his King. A final move by my Knight clinched the matter. A queer smile played over my lips as I looked up at him, straight into his eyes, and said ever so softly, "Check and mate, sir."

My eyes glittered with pleasure as Lawrence, after a few moments of silence, gently lifted his conquered King in long, slender fingers and laid it on its side. He sat back in his chair, his fingers lightly touching his pursed lips.

The firelight danced about us, creating fanciful

shadows and eerie lights on his face. Finally he said in a slow, thoughtful voice, "A well-played game, my dear. Victory tastes sweet, does it not?"

I turned my head slightly, so that my face was in the shadows. My voice was tense with suppressed excitement. "Of a certainty it does, my lord. Could victory ever be otherwise?"

The oddest smile flitted across his face as he agreed, "No, of course not. But do you not agree that the most important of victories, the sweetest by far, is the ultimate victory, the total devastation of the adversary?"

My sense of elation faltered. I did not answer, for I was unsure of how to interpret his words. I did not dare chance exposing myself by bandying words with him.

Lawrence began to gather the chess pieces into the center of the table. He righted his fallen King and placed it in front of the black pieces, on the square directly opposite my Queen. He looked up into my face, his eyes narrowed and grim. I met his gaze steadily. It was he who looked away first, into the fire, and then down at his shapely white hands. I nervously plucked at the heavy folds of my gown. When he finally spoke, his voice was soft, almost pensive. "You played with intelligence, finesse, and, yes, courage, Andrea. Most unusual characteristics for a woman."

"I was not aware, my lord, that men were the sole proprietors of intelligence and courage," I replied with quiet dignity.

He sighed. "Ah, my dear, there you are wrong, and I think that you must perforce bow to my superior years of experience in the matter." He continued, his voice cold now and cutting, like a rapier through the silent air, "Oh, yes, your sex is weak, vain, and totally lacking in moral character!"

Angrily and without thought to my precarious position, I rose quickly to my feet and leaned across the chess table and said in a mocking, icy voice, "Those are words of a bitter man, my lord, words that lack both measure and a balanced judgment. No, my lord," I added scornfully, "even your years of experience cannot justify such an unbalanced opinion!"

He jerked forward in one swift movement, grabbed my wrist in a painful grip, and pulled me toward him so that my face was very close to his. "Brave words, my girl," he hissed, "but words without substance, without meaning. Ah, yes, you silly creature, you can taste fleeting victory at a game of chess, for you were well-taught." His grip tightened. "But in life, Andrea, in life you have been but a miserable pawn in a game of my own making! And now I have what I want, my girl, and I no longer need you; I no longer need to pander to your foolish whims and childish desires."

"You are mad, sir!" I cried, trying to pull free of his hand, but his grip remained, unyielding. Pain shot up my arm, but I made no sound.

"Mad, am I? We shall see my girl!" Abruptly he released my wrist and fastened his long fingers around my throat in one swift motion. I instinctively grabbed at his hands to free myself, but his hold tightened inexorably. "You shall see, my dear, that you are quite helpless. And never forget," he added with a marked sneer, "that you belong to me, wife. You are naught but my property—to do with as I choose." There was emphasis on each word.

As I felt myself grow faint from want of air, he did the unexpected. He released his hold from around my throat and moved his hands to capture my face tightly between his palms. Before I realized what he intended, he had pulled me quickly against him. I felt his hot breath upon my face. To my horror, he pressed his lips against mine. I struggled wildly but vainly, trying to pull free. His response was to hold me more tightly and to grind his mouth against mine, so that finally my bruised lips parted and I felt his tongue against my teeth.

As abruptly as he had begun his assault, he released me and flung me from him. I would have sprawled to the floor had my chair not been directly behind me. He swept away the chess table with one violent motion, sending the pieces flying in every direction. He stood over me with his legs spread and his hands on his hips.

"I find your actions despicable, sir!" I cried, filled with humiliation and disgust. "I would make you pay for this if I were a man!"

"Most inappropriate that I should desire a man, my dear," he lashed back sarcastically.

I exploded. "You sicken me, my lord. I find you repellent."

I thought that he would strike me, so suffused with anger and fury did his face become. But he regained control, and after staring at me intently for a long moment, said in a soft, meditative voice, as if he were thinking aloud, "How strange that I have never before noticed. You really are a remarkably beautiful woman" . . . . His voice trailed off, and he reached out his hand toward me.

I shrank back in unspeakable horror, swept by revulsion and fear, for his eyes seemed to strip me naked.

He jerked himself back and withdrew his hand. He addressed me in a voice of deadly calm. "I have decided to assert my rights as a husband. You are, after all, my wife, Andrea, and thus subject to my will."

"You . . . you cannot mean that!" I felt dizziness and nausea flood over me. In a voice that I hardly recognized as my own, I said in a strangled whisper, "You promised . . . you signed your promise in the marriage contract. You are my husband in name only!" My voice had risen to a pitch of hysteria.

"Oh, that." He shrugged his shoulders contemptuously. "What nonsense! What can that possibly have to do with my wishes now? 'Tis but a worthless piece of paper, designed merely to calm your anxieties, so that, my dear, you would consent to this marriage!"

"Oh, God, no, please no," I cried piteously.

"All women are whores at heart, my dear. You cannot be that unlike the rest of your sex!"

My lips moved, but there was no sound. My eyes were focused upon his face, but I no longer saw him. Frightful images arose in my mind, images that I had tried so desperately to forget. I found myself being drawn inexorably back—back into time. I saw myself as a child of eight. I was in my father's study, curled up behind a heavily curtained window seat, dozing over the book I had found. I was awakened suddenly by low throaty laughter and strange sounds. I peered hesitantly out of my hiding place and saw my father and a parlour maid locked in a tight embrace. I remained silent and unobserved, uncertain what to do, but realizing somehow that I should not be there. There were cries, but not cries of pain, and low, animallike noises. The maid, Molly, lay on her back, her full skirts flung up about her face, my father with his breeches unbuttoned, driving between her uplifted legs that horrible erect mound of flesh . . . the pounding, the moaning, the distorted faces . . . I stuffed my fist in my mouth to keep from gagging. Animals—they were like the horses heaving and grunting in the field . . . .

My mother's pale, wan face appeared before my eyes. She was strangely silent, dark shadows under her eyes. I heard her yelling at my father of her shame, and I felt her hatred of him and of Molly.

My mother's face was drowned by Molly's screams. I was in the servants' quarters, drawn by the incessant animal screams. I saw her gross, heaving body, her back arched up and her face distorted. They pulled a small, limp, bloody object from between her legs. Then there was blood, fountains of gushing, spurting blood, covering the bed, dripping onto the wooden floor. My fingers were sticky red, the blood all over me, covering my clothing. Now they were screaming, rushing frantically, stuffing sheets between Molly's legs. But Molly didn't scream. Her head lolled lifeless to the side of the bed, vacant glazed eyes staring . . . .

I ran my tongue over my dry lips. If only I could forget the blood, dripping silently to the floor . . . a red-purple pool! My tortured mind flew to my mother, my beautiful mother. She was so stiff, so cold to the touch, so white . . . .

"Oh, my God . . . he killed her, he killed them all . . . ," I sobbed.

"Andrea, Andrea!"

I was jerked suddenly from the grim images at the repeated sound of my name. I was moaning aloud. I looked up dazedly into my husband's face.

His eyes narrowed as he gazed intently at my blanched face. My body was trembling. I felt so foolish, but I could not control it! I rubbed my hand vigorously across my forehead, trying to banish the past back into its place.

The silence seemed endless, but it did not really matter, for I was too concerned trying to vanquish my own personal nightmare.

"Perhaps I understand why you married me, Andrea." His voice was hard, scornful.

My eyes flew to his. Had I spoken aloud? Had I moaned aloud those frightening images?

"You thought I would take your grandfather's place, did you not? That I would protect you and keep you safe from your own fears?" I gasped as he added maliciously, "There is no place for a lusty young husband in your plans, is there, Andrea?"

John, oh, John. A knife turned in my heart. I shook my head mutely.

"Someday, if there is to be a someday, you must tell me more of your past . . . and of your father." His hard, cold voice rang in my ears.

"My father? What . . . . what do you mean?" I cried

"No matter now. It is really of no importance." He added with a sneer, "You will learn that I know more of your past than you realize."

"I . . . I don't understand," I stammered, completely at sea.

"You will soon enough," he replied brusquely. He leaned down over me, his face close to mine. I shrank back instinctively, pressing my back hard against the chair. He straightened abruptly and gave a short mocking laugh. "You need not fear that I will rape you! Terrified virgins are not to my liking!"

A hysterical sob broke from my throat. "Then what do you intend?" I asked hoarsely.

He did not immediately reply, but sat down in his chair, his arms folded across his chest. "You really were quite stupid in your search of my rooms," he remarked.

My mind refused to function, and I stared at him blankly.

He reached into the pocket of his waistcoat, drew out the bent hairpin, and held it up for me to see. "Really quite stupid, my girl!" he mocked.

He knew! Oh, God, he knew what I had done! I shook my head, a denial on my lips.

"No, don't bother to deny it, my dear! You left it most conveniently for me to find on top of the desk." He began twirling the bent hairpin between his long fingers. The cruel smile changed to a triumphant gleam.

What a fool I was! I had even bungled my search of his rooms! I felt drained, defeated. At least now there seemed to be no reason why I should not know why he was doing this.

"Tell me why you have done this, Lawrence. Is it not my right to know?"

"Rights? Rights? You have no rights, madam!" he said brutally. Then, in a milder tone he added, "You will find out all in good time, my dear, never fear."

He stood up abruptly, interrupting my frantic thoughts. "Enough of this! I really have no more time to waste on you tonight, my girl. It is time you went to your room, but do not doubt that I will deal with you soon enough."

He took my arm and pulled me, unresisting, to my feet. "Do you choose to come with me quietly?"

I looked up into his cold steel-gray eyes. "I will come with you quietly, my lord," I affirmed with as much dignity as I could muster.

"Remember," he reminded me sharply as he opened the doors to the drawing room, "no heroics or screams; never doubt that the servants would obey me instantly! . . . You are doing fine, my dear," he hissed in my ear as we silently passed a footman at the top landing.

As we neared my room, my thoughts flew to Belinda. She would be waiting for me!

It was if he read my mind, "Incidentally, Andrea, your maid will not be in your room."

I had not time to respond, for he opened the door to the Blue Room, released my arm, and pushed me inside. I whirled around and looked at him standing in the open doorway.

"Do not worry that I will forget you, my dear." With those words he closed the door. I heard the key turn in the lock.

EIGHT

The bitter winter wind numbed my face and whipped mercilessly at my tight-fitting woolen cap. I leaned close to Trojan's neck to suck in the warmth of his steaming mane. Already his breathing was laboured and his flanks lathered from his unremitting pace. His great body heaved and trembled beneath me, and I slowed him for fear he would collapse. I guided him carefully into copse off the main road, slid from his back, and pulled the reins over his head. He tossed his head, flecks of foam whirling from his mouth onto my gloves. After I rubbed down his back and flanks with the saddle blanket, I spread it over him to protect him as best I could from the cold winter wind.

The wind billowed my cloak as I walked slowly back to the main road and peered intently in the direction we had come. The pale winter moon glittered down on the empty expanse of road. A lone owl hooted his presence as I sank down to my knees in the bushes near Trojan and pressed against the naked limbs for warmth. A pain shot through my ankle. I sat back quickly, withdrew my legs from beneath me, and began to massage my ankle as best I could through my boot. I winced from the smarting in my ankle as well as from the memory of my precarious situation. I had stood numbly in the middle of my room, staring at the locked door, listening to Lawrence's retreating footsteps.

My initial reaction was to pound the door and scream for help. I ran to the door, my hands formed into fists, then I stopped short. There was no one to hear me! Of course, I realized, this was why Lawrence had insisted that I have the Blue Room! I was alone in the west wing, effectively cut off from the rest of the family and servants—a prisoner. I seemed to lose all will, and I felt a cold emptiness and lethargy numb my body and creep into my mind. I sank down to the carpet and slumped forward, my forehead pressed against my outstretched arms. Suddenly I jerked myself up. I would not give up and wait, helpless and frightened, for my husband to come for me. The bell cord! I jumped to my feet and ran to my bed, only to find that the bell cord had been neatly cut and now hung useless. I grabbed the cord and yanked at it furiously. Had my husband thought of everything? Slowly I dropped the tasseled cord. My eyes traveled around the room and came to rest but a moment later on the curtained windows. I rushed to the windows, pulled back the heavy curtains, and peered out into the darkness. I unlatched a window, pushed it open, and leaned out over the casement. The drop to the ground was too great a distance, and the outer walls seemed sheer. The bitter wind stung my eyes as my fingers probed along the casement. There was a ledge, a narrow ledge that extended beyond the reach of my arm.

Trojan gave a sudden snort and pawed the ground. I

jumped stiffly to my feet and ran to the road. I stood frozen for a moment listening, but no sound reached my ears.

Trojan seemed rested, his breathing even, his body tense and ready. As I quickly smoothed the blanket and hauled the saddle back onto his back, I wondered whether Lawrence had discovered my escape and was not, at this moment, riding hard after me. My anxiety communicated itself to Trojan, and he tossed his head around as if to encourage me to hurry. Finally, saddle in place, I grasped the pommel and pulled myself up on his back. We regained the main road, and Trojan, with little encouragement from me, broke into a steady, long-strided gallop. I leaned down again and rubbed the throbbing ankle, thankful that I had escaped with such a slight injury. It could have been much worse.

The ledge was narrow, dangerously narrow, and I did not even know where it led. But it seemed the only way, and I had to try. I pulled back into the room and looked down at my heavy velvet gown. A dress would never do. If I was to make my way along the ledge, I could not be encumbered with woman's skirts. I rushed to my wardrobe and searched through the bottom drawers until I found my boy's breeches that I had worn as a girl in Yorkshire. What better disguise than to travel as a boy, safe from prying, curious eyes! I quickly gathered together the rest of my costume—a tight woolen cap to hide my long hair, boots, and a shirt. I was fastening my cloak when I realized that I must have money for my journey. I found only a few odd shillings in my drawer. I grabbed a handful of jewelry to supplement this meager supply, stuffing bracelets and rings into the pocket of my voluminous cloak.

Exactly where I would go, I determined to figure out later. First I had to somehow make my way to the ground. I stepped an uncertain boot onto the ledge and steadied myself by gripping the open window frame. I took a deep breath, pressed hard against the stone, and focused my eyes on the narrow ledge before me. I saw it disappear around a corner. My gloved hands clung tightly to the rough edges of the stone as, inch my inch, I slid my feet toward the corner. Beads of perspiration broke out on my forehead, only to be whipped into my eyes, nearly blinding me, by the howling wind.

I gained the corner and pulled myself around it slowly, only to discover that the ledge ended abruptly. In its place stood the outjutting outline of a massive chimney. To my unbounded relief, the stones were not fitted smoothly against each other, but protruded irregularly, just enough, I hoped, to afford me a firm grip. As my fingers closed around the stone edges, I swung my legs off the ledge, and for one long moment I dangled in midair until my feet found furrowed edges for support.

My descent was painfully slow, and several times I hung by my arms as my boots sought a hold. Suddenly, as I loosed my grip to find another hold, the stone crumbled beneath my feet and I hurtled to the ground. My legs twisted under me as I fell sprawling on my side. I lay still for a moment as a stabbing pain shot up my leg. I prayed that my leg was not broken. I rose slowly, flexed the leg, and discovered that it was fine but that I had wrenched my ankle.

I was drawn back to the present by pinpoints of light in the distance. It was a village. I wondered if I dared risk riding into the village to trade Trojan for another mount. I was still not far enough from Devbridge Manor, and Lawrence was well-known in these parts, as was his horse, Trojan. If his horse were recognized, I would be taken for a thief and soon enough my identity as a woman discovered. No, it was not worth the risk. I would simply have to ride Trojan to the next village or a farmhouse.

I slowed Trojan and looked about for the best route to skirt the village. An open field presented itself, and Trojan sailed over the low fence with little effort. Once beyond the village, we veered back onto the main road. Our long ride continued, the silence broken rhythmically by the steady pounding of Trojan's hooves. I thought wryly of the look on Craigsdale's face when I would arrive in London and present myself at his door. "Balmy" Craigsdale, as Peter called him, Grandfather's solicitor since before I was born. I could think of no one more trustworthy than Craigsdale. I felt certain that he would hide me until Peter's return.

My thought were suspended as I realized that my chance of reaching London might very well depend on the small stable boy, Jem.

I was dismayed when I chanced to look up as I saddled Trojan, to see the boy standing motionless, staring at me mutely. The both of us stood eyeing each other cautiously. I took a step toward him, and he backed away, tugging fiercely at the red shock of hair on his forehead.

" 'Tis all right, Jem," I coaxed, a knot forming in the pit of my stomach at his unexpected presence. "You see, I could not sleep," I began soothingly. "Like you, evidently," I added as he took another step backward, his small body poised for flight.

"Now, Jem, there is no reason for you to be frightened and wake anyone. I am riding out for but a little while and shall be back quite soon, you will see. Everything is fine, I assure you." I spoke with much more calm than I felt. With nervous fingers that seemed not to want to do my bidding, I slowly fastened the saddle girth into place. Jem continued staring, his mouth agape, uncertain of what he should do.

"You be a good boy and go back to bed," I commanded gently as I led Trojan from his stall.

Gloomily I wondered if Jem had awakened Billy or one of the other grooms. The child was unpredictable, and there was no way of knowing if he believed me or even understood me.

Foaming saliva was dripping now from Trojan's mouth and his eyes were wild with fatigue. I realized that if I pushed him further, I would kill him. I reined him in, slipped from his back, and began stroking his trembling head tenderly. I had no choice now; I had to find a farmhouse and trade him for another mount.

I continued on foot, leading him. There seemed to be naught but the never-ending road and trees. My pulses quickened at the sight of a small farmhouse in the distance. "Come, Trojan," I urged, tugging at his reins. "You will soon rest."

At that moment Trojan stopped in his tracks, threw back his head, and whinnied, I stood frozen, my ears straining to hear. Had a bird or an animal frightened him? I clamped my fingers down on his nostrils. He could not be allowed to whinny again. The two of us remained motionless in tense silence, waiting.

I could feel the vibration of the horses' hooves against my feet before I actually heard them. There were several riders, and they were coming nearer! I frantically jerked at Trojan's reins and pulled him off the road into a clump of trees. I clutched his nostrils more firmly. I could not allow him to betray our presence.

The horses slowed, and I could hear mens' voices. They had heard Trojan whinny the first time! I clung to Trojan, feeling him tense.

Trojan, a loyal animal, recognized his master's voice. Despite my firm hold, he tore loose, raised his head proudly, and neighed loudly.

I heard shouts. Grabbing Trojan's reins, I threw myself up onto his back and wheeled him around. We shot from the trees onto the road like a cannonball.

It was a desperate chase, but I knew that I had no chance. Trojan heaved and groaned beneath me, each stride a tremendous effort. Tears of frustration and despair rolled down my cheeks, only to become cold silent drops, like hard rain against my face. I looked over my shoulder once and could make out my husband's grim face in the pale dawn light. I was fairly choking with fear.

It was but a moment later that a horse was beside me and a strong arm shot out and encircled my body. I was lifted wildly kicking from Trojan's back, the reins torn loose from my hands. There was a coarse pockmarked face above me. With every shred of energy left to me, I fought, hitting at the grinning face, clawing at the arm that held me.

Abruptly I was released and lowered to the ground. Another strong hand grabbed my arm in a firm grip and I was whirled roughly around, to see my husband's cold, set face above mine. I continued to struggle. In an angry voice I heard Lawrence cry, "If you do not stop fighting me, I will break your arm!" His grip tightened to prove his point. I gasped with sudden pain and ceased my struggle.

"Freesen, get my horse!" Lawrence shouted to the pockmarked man.

I stood panting, my face pressed against the sleeve of Lawrence's greatcoat. I saw Jarrell, my husband's valet, from the corner of my eyes. He had dismounted and stood silently beside us, his face expressionless. I saw that their horses were fresh and free of sweat. They must have changed them in the village. If only I had dared the risk, I might still be free.

Lawrence turned back to me. His lips were pursed and his eyes narrowed. "Well, madam, the race is over!"

"Only this race, my lord," I retorted, thrusting my chin up aggressively.

He gave a short, grim laugh. "It is true that I underestimated your resourcefulness. You might even have escaped had I not thought to take a draught to your room to ensure your night's sleep. But not again, my dear, not again!"

"What happens now, my lord—will you bar the windows again as they were for Lady Caroline?" I mocked him. What did I have to lose?

In that instant, I recoiled, certain that he would strike. His flattened hand was in midair and his face was suffused with anger.

"My lord!" Jarrell's voice cut through the tension.

Slowly Lawrence lowered his hand. He gave my arm another wrench, and in spite of myself, a low moan escaped my lips.

"Do not provoke me again, madam," he hissed as he flung me away from him. I staggered, tried in vain to retain my balance, and fell in a heap at Jarrell's feet.

"Watch her!" he snarled to Jarrell.

"Well, man, what of my horse?" He strode away to Freesen.

"It's blown, he is, my lord. Fairly ridden him into the ground, she 'as!"

"Damnation!" He wheeled around to face me, his jaw working angrily. "You will pay dearly for this night's work, madam!"

He regained control of himself after a moment and said shortly to Freesen, "Lead him, Freesen. We will have to proceed slowly."

I remained on my knees on the cold ground, rubbing my forearm vigorously.

Jarrell knelt down next to me and inquired in an anxious voice, "Is your ladyship's arm all right?"

I merely nodded. I felt wretched and numb from the

cold and dread of what would happen, but I would not let them see my fear.

"Let me help you to rise, my lady," Jarrell offered, his tone more neutral.

"Very well." I sighed, allowing the valet to assist me to my feet.

Lawrence completed his examination to Trojan and returned with a meaningful stride over to us. My legs were trembling, but the devil, I thought, I would not let him know how afraid I was.

"What is our destination now, my lord?" I asked quite conversationally.

"That you will find out soon enough, ma'am," he replied shortly.

"Freesen!" He beckoned the other man to come over to us. "Toss her up onto Trojan and tie her hands securely to the pommel!"

"Surely, my lord—" Jarrell began, his eyes darting anxiously from my drawn face to his master's.

"Enough, man, she deserves to be flung facedown over the saddle! I am being overgenerous in my treatment!" Lawrence cried impatiently.

"I have never done aught to harm you, Lawrence," I said evenly, my eyes searching his face.

"You have thwarted me, madam, and you have meddled. I will tolerate neither!"

"And were you being overgenerous when you placed the barbed circle of wire under Dante's saddle?" I cried, anger flaring.

"It served its purpose," he replied indifferently.

"You are contemptible . . . I hope that you rot in hell!" I spat the words at him. Freesen was holding my arms, winding rope around my hands, so there was no way I could protect myself when the blow fell. Lawrence hit me with his fist against my head. The force of the blow sent me staggering against Freesen's chest. Strange lights exploded in my head and blurred my vision. Everything went mercifully black.

I was aware of the horse's rhythmic motion before I fully regained consciousness. When I finally managed to force my eyes open, the world began to spin weirdly around me. Dizziness and nausea flooded over me and I closed my eyes tightly and swallowed convulsively. I must have moved, for I heard Jarrell's voice right behind me. "Please do not move, my lady. I will keep you steady."

I became aware that his arm was about me and that I sagged against his chest. At that moment I stupidly remembered that other time, so long ago, it seemed, when I had leaned gratefully and trustingly against John's chest.

I said nothing to Jarrell until I had gained firm control over my queasy stomach. The side of my head ached abominably.

"Where are we bound, Jarrell?" I finally inquired.

"I . . . I really cannot say, my lady." He hesitated.

"It is all right, Jarrell." I sighed. "I would not wish you also to be in the earl's bad graces."

"My lady," Jarrel whispered, his head close to my ear, "I tried to convince his lordship that his quarrel was not with you . . . but to no avail."

"Then who is his quarrel with, Jarrell?" I asked sharply.

He made no immediate response.

I pursued, "With my father?"

He took a sharp intake of breath. "Please, my lady," he begged, "I must not—indeed, I cannot—speak of this matter further!" He was agitated and clearly afraid of his master.

We rode on in silence, Freesen and my husband some little distance ahead of us. The sun was rising high in the sky; it was late morning. I thought dully that we must be nearing Devbridge Manor. Everything had been for naught.

To my surprise, our cavalcade turned off the main road onto a rutted, narrow path. I turned my head and looked questioningly at Jarrell. He shook his head and looked resolutely ahead. Soon a small cottage appeared. Smoke gushed from the chimney, and I saw a horse tethered to a tree beside the door.

Lawrence reined in beside us. "Ah, madam, I see that you are awake. It is good of you to oblige me in such good time!" His voice was carefree and gay. I frowned, not understanding how my being conscious just now obliged him.

We pulled up in front of the rude dwelling, and Lawrence lifted me down. I would have fallen had he not held me firmly by the arms.

"Steady, now, my dear," he prompted. "I would not want you to faint now, when I have such a surprise for you!" I glanced briefly into his face. His eyes glittered with suppressed excitement.

"What do you mean?" I demanded, puzzled.

He gave a short laugh and commanded Freesen to open the door.

Lawrence guided me firmly into the cottage. It was dark inside, and it took a moment for my eyes to adjust. A rough-looking man stepped forward and nodded to Lawrence. A miserable fire burned in the grate, and there were rough chairs and a table set around it. My eyes traveled to the far corner of the room. Against the far wall stood a cot, and on it lay a man, half-covered with a filthy blanket.

"Come, madam, surely you do not wish to be backward in your attentions!"

Lawrence pressed his hand against the small of my back and propelled me forward.

The man stirred, moaned softly, and then pulled himself up painfully on one elbow. He stared at us vacantly, puzzled.

I started back. My heart began to pound wildly. My hand flew to my mouth to stifle a cry. Ten years rolled away. There in front of me was my father! There was only slight white in his still-golden hair. Lines of dissipation were etched into his cheeks, but he was still handsome. Bright, bright blue eyes stared at me unknowingly.

"Well, Jameson, see what I have brought you!" Lawrence's voice was joyous, elated. There was no response from my father.

"What do you say, man?" Lawrence shouted.

I suppose it was at that moment that Lawrence realized that my father was gazing unknowingly at a slender boy in a long black cloak and tight-fitting cap.

Lawrence tore the cap from my head, and my hair spilled out over my shoulders and down my back.

My father gave a hoarse cry. "Oh, my God! You devil . . . you devil, I'll kill you for this!" My father leaped at Lawrence, but Freesen and the other man, Dykes, quickly stepped in the way and shoved him back; he fell gasping with pain onto the cot.

My father sagged back against the wall and then struggled forward, lifting his face to mine.

"Andrea, Andrea, oh, my poor child! I can never forgive myself for this!" His voice was hoarse and low. His eyes pleaded, and he slowly extended his hands out toward me.

I still stood rooted to the floor, mute. It was like looking into a mirror, so much alike were we. I thought briefly of my mother. How strange it was that neither of her children even resembled her. Finally, in a queer, distant voice I whispered, "Father?"

Lawrence laughed, a mocking, cruel laugh. "So she recognized you, Jameson. I wondered if she would!"

Again my father tried to lunge for him, and again Freesen pushed him back violently. I heard him gasp in pain. A small bright red spot appeared at his shoulder and began to spread. He was wounded! His fine cambric shirt was in tatters, his breeches dirty and caked with mud.

"Father, you are hurt!"

I made a move toward him, but my husband grabbed my arm and held me fast.

"Do not worry, wife, I placed the bullet well. I would not have him die too quickly!"

I looked in anguish from Lawrence to my father and back again. My bewildered face came to rest on my husband's.

"Will you now tell me, my lord, what you have against my father? What has he done to deserve such treatment at your hand?"

Lawrence turned to my father, his eyes gleaming with hatred. "Well, Jameson, do you tell her, or do I?"

My father seemed to regain control over himself, for he answered calmly enough, "It is not her affair, Devbridge. Leave it between us."

"Hardly, sir," he snarled. His lips were drawn over his teeth in a thin line. "After all, it is only through her that I could get to you. And, as you see, I have succeeded!" His voice was triumphant.

"Please, sir, in this he is right," I pleaded. "It seems that I am not only the instrument of his revenge but also a victim. Have I not a right to know?" I did not add, "since I will probably die," but the unspoken thought hung in the air, a grim reality all the same.

My father sighed deeply, shifted his weight, and looked down at his hands. When he finally lifted his head, his eyes pierced deeply into mine, and in them was written pain and despair.

"Father . . . please," I urged.

He seemed now not to see me, and his eyes fastened to a spot beyond me. In a weary, beaten voice, he began, "It was such a long time ago . . ." He halted, shaken by a spasm of coughing. The room was painfully quiet save for his racked cough.

He wiped his sleeve across his mouth, and then, slowly, his eyes holding mine, he spoke. "I met Lady Caroline in Paris. She was at the time Devbridge's . . . second wife."

My mouth was dry, so dry that I could hardly breathe. I pressed my hand against my lips, knowing even now what he would say.

In an almost inaudible voice he said, "We became . . . lovers. Oh, my God, Andrea," he cried suddenly, "you must try to understand, to forgive me!"

"Pray continue, Jameson," Lawrence hurled harshly at him. "It is time she knew the whole truth about her father!"

"Very well," my father responded, his voice sad and tired. "You shall hear it all. Lady Caroline became with child. I, of course, was married to your mother. I assumed that she would simply pass the child off as the earl's. It was then that she informed me that she had been traveling—without her husband—for well over three months. There was no way the child could be his."

He got no further in his grim recital, for I fairly shrieked at him, "You killed Lady Caroline, just as you killed my mother . . . just as you killed poor Molly!"

"Molly?" he repeated blankly.

"Do you not even remember all of your mistresses?" I cried, feeling myself being dragged back into that awful nightmare.

His face cleared. "You mean the housemaid who died in childbed?"

"Yes, with your child!" My voice was now leaden. My

hatred for him was like a living thing in the room I did not even realize that we were not alone.

"Andrea, you were but a child. You could not possibly understand . . ." he pleaded.

I stood rigid, lost for a long moment in the past, my mother's wan, tearful face passing before my eyes. Ten years ago . . . my mother was dead, buried, gone. A door closed in my mind. I looked into those bright blue eyes —my eyes—and whispered, "Why did you leave me, Father? Why did you go without a word? Why did you leave me alone?"

He replied in a voice full of bitterness and regret, "I was forced to leave, my child. Your grandfather would not allow me to be near you, and," he added with finality, "Devbridge would have killed me had I stayed."

The door to the past remained closed, forever closed now. I gazed at him intently, perhaps not fully understanding, but now that we were about to die, it did not seem to matter. My father had returned, and we were together. I stretched out my hand to him. "Did you come to save me, Father?" I asked gently.

"Yes," he replied simply, taking my hand in both of his. Lawrence made no move to stop us.

I moved slowly to him and sat down beside him on the rude cot. I would comfort him, but first I had to know the rest. "It seems that we are in this situation together, Father. You owe it to me, I must know the rest."

His eyes wavered from my face. "There is not much more, Andrea. Caroline left Paris to return to Devbridge, for she had no other choice." He motioned with disdain toward Lawrence. "I found that Devbridge took her back immediately to Devbridge Manor and spread the story that she was mad. It is my belief that after the child was born he murdered her!"

I reeled back in shock. Lawrence executed a slight, mocking bow. "How very acute of you, my dear Jameson.

Of course, the slut did not deserve to be the Countess of Devbridge! She was a wanton whore and got her just deserts!"

Judith! Judith was my father's daughter—my half-sister! No wonder she had always seemed so familiar to me! "Father." I cried, my voice breaking, "you have a daughter . . . Judith!"

"Yes, I know. Andrea. I have always known, but there was little I could do about it." His voice was leaden.

I wheeled on Lawrence. He was regarding us intently, a broad smile on his face. "Do you not wonder, my dear, why I let the child, Judith, live? The fruit of a whore and your father?"

I could not answer, for there were no words.

He broke into an ugly laugh. "Well, I will tell you both. Every time I looked at the child, I thought of you, Jameson, and how I would savor my revenge. Caroline's death was but half of my vengeance!"

"You . . . you would not harm the child, would you?" I gasped, shrinking closer to my father. His hands tightened around mine.

He ignored my question, and seeing me recoil from him, cried harshly, "Ah, do not think that he can protect you, madam!"

He moved quickly forward and grabbed my arm to pull me from my father. In that second my wounded father, with almost unbelievable strength, lunged toward him and grabbed his throat between his two hands. Freesen and Dykes were on him in an instant, but they could not pull him away. I looked wildly around for some sort of weapon, anything to help my father, for they would surely overcome him in but a moment.

The moment came too soon. As my father was torn away, Lawrence, with a yell of fury, grabbed up one of the wooden chairs and brought it down with all his weight against my father's head. Freesen and Dykes let go of him instinctively and he slumped with a heavy thud to the floor. Blood flowed from his face and head. I hurled myself to the floor beside him. "Father, Father," I cried, shaking his shoulders, trying frantically but uselessly to awaken him. I touched his bloodied, distorted face, the blood-matted hair. His sightless blue eyes stared up at me, unblinking, lifeless. Tears streamed heedlessly down my face, falling onto his, mixing with the blood.

"No, Father," I moaned, "please don't leave me now. Please, Father . . ." I kept pushing and tugging at his limp body, willing him to come back to me, refusing to believe that he was dead. He was dead, dead like my mother. He had left me again, now gone forever.

Lawrence's voice broke into my shocked grief. "God damn his soul to hell! He has died much too quickly and easily!" He sounded furious.

Something snapped inside me. In a wild fury I leaped up and jumped at him. My attack was unexpected, and my nails dug mercilessly down his cheeks. I could feel his skin tear under my neals, and then the warmth of his blood on my fingers.

He howled with pain and anger. My attack was short-lived, for as my fists pounded at his face, his fingers went around my throat. I pulled wildly at his hands, but it was to no avail. My eyes began to bulge and my tongue thickened in my mouth.

I was about to die! In that moment I saw my father's tired, pleading face, asking my forgiveness, but his face blurred and dissolved into my husband's hate-filled eyes.

I heard Jarrell's distraught voice from what seemed a great distance pleading over and over, "No, my lord, stop . . . you must not do this!"

The cruel fingers slowly loosened their hold. There came another voice, a voice I knew, cutting like steel and ice through the air. "Do as Jarrell says, Father, or I will put a bullet through your shoulder!"

The fingers dropped instantly from my throat and I fell backward onto the floor, my back hitting against the cot. My breath reteurned in short, painful gasps. The voice I knew—John's voice—reached my ears over my pained breathing. "Andrea, are you all right? Andrea!"

I slowly focused on the strange scene before my eyes. John stood framed in the doorway, Ferguson just behind him. He held a pistol in his hand. Lawrence, Jarrell, and the other two men stood motionless, their eyes on John.

"Andrea?" he repeated sharply, as I gazed at him dazedly.

"Yes, I am all right," I croaked, my fingers tentatively rubbing my bruised throat.

Lawrence still stood mute, the deep slashes from my nails standing bright red on his white face. A sob caught in my throat as I looked at my father's bloodied body. I tore my gaze away.

"John . . . how are you here?" My voice rasped unnaturally in the tense silence.

"My only problem was in finding you, Andrea. I am but sorry that I arrived too late." His eyes left my face and rested briefly on my father's body.

Lawrence seemed to shake himself loose of his shock. He gave a brittle laugh. "Well, my son . . . what now?"

"Exactly what is to be done after your . . . morning's work, I have yet to determine." He shook his head slowly. "You are insane, Father, quite insane."

Lawrence's face blazed with sudden anger. H took an uncertain step toward his son, seemed to think better of it, and stopped. "How dare you speak like that to me, you ungrateful . . ." His voice was momentarily suspended in his own fury.

"Ungrateful? No, Father!" he flung back at him. "I guessed what you had done to Caroline, Father, but I did not then betray you. Did you never guess why I willingly left my home and spent all those years in the army? I could not stay in the some house with you! No, Father, I did not betray you, but now I see that I was wrong. You could not be content with one person's blood on your conscience!"

"Don't you preach to me of betrayal!" Lawrence exploded. "She was a whore and a trollop and merited death!" He drew himself up and continued in a deadly calm voice, "You are no longer my son. I want never to set eyes on you again." He turned his eyes toward me and waved a disdainful arm. "You want her? Take her . . . you're welcome to the slut! At least," he spat, "I have relieved you of her worthless father!"

I gasped in fury and staggered to my feet. "Father was right . . . you are a devil!" I started forward, my hands outstretched toward his face. "Murderer!"

"Andrea, stop!" John's command cut through my unreasoning anger, and I halted, weaving uncertainly. "Come here, Andrea." He extended his arm toward me.

I took a deep, sobbing breath and went to him. He caught me in his arms, and I leaned against him, my head resting against his shoulder. His arms tightened and his lips brushed lightly against my hair.

In that instant a shot rang out, and John's arm jerked away from me. His pistol went spinning to the floor. I cried out as John grabbed his arm. Blood welled up between his fingers through his rent shirt.

"Forgive me, Andrea," he said grimly, his face drawn in lines of frustration and pain.

"Most affecting!" Lawrence mocked, now sure of himself, as he directed the still-smoking pistol at us.

John straightened and stood quietly, watching his father. "Well, Father, it appears that you have your way for the moment. What do you intend to do?"

Lawrence regarded his son disdainfully, ignoring his question. "It was amusing, dear boy, to watch you fall in love with her. So very common of you," he mused.

"Then you do not know your son, my lord, for you have not at all understood his feelings! It is Lady Elizabeth he loves," I protested.

John turned to me, a disquieting smile lighting his eyes. "No, my love, it is you who are quite wrong. I have loved you even though you were my father's wife."

"Enough!" came Lawrence's harsh voice.

I looked up at his words, to see him level the pistol at his son. Ferguson tried to move forward, but John stopped him.

"That's right, dear boy," Lawrence sneered, "hold your man."

Jarrell cried, "You cannot, my lord. Not your own son!"

"Shut up, you fool! Surely you must realize that there can be no witnesses!"

John shoved me firmly behind him and shielded my body with his. He made a final attempt. "Let her go, sir, she has done nothing to merit your revenge."

"You have never been a dutiful son," Lawrence remarked as he cocked the pistol.

"You are mad!" I cried.

Again a burst of fire exploded in the small room, rending the silence. I jumped forward, my arms going around John. To my surprise, he did not fall against me.

I looked at Lawrence, to see him frowning at his son. The frown froze on his face, and he fell slowly forward and slumped to the floor.

"I couldn't let him do it, Master Jack!" Jarrell stood like a stricken man behind his dead master, a pistol dangling loosely from his hand.

John pulled himself loose from my arms and walked to where Jarrell stood and took the pistol from his hand.

Jarrell looked up at him with anguished eyes.

"You saved our lives, Jarrell," John said softly.

"He changed, my lord. He did not used to be so," he said dully, his face a white mask. "His desire for revenge unbalanced his mind. I realized it fully when he . . . acted so toward her ladyship."

John responded gently, "We must all try to forget this, Jarrell. You have done the right thing. I thank you most sincerely."

John turned to Freesen and Dykes, who stood tensed and ready, their eyes measuring the distance to the doorway.

"I don't know who either of you are, but I presume that you have long been in his lordship's employ."

"No, milord," Freesen whined, "and we didn't know his lordship was going to kill anybody."

John interrupted sternly, "I am certain that you have been sufficiently involved to merit the magistrate's interest." He paused a moment to let his words take effect before he continued smoothly. "However, I am prepared to let both of you go, provided that neither of you ever shows himself again. Do I make myself perfectly clear?"

"Aye, milord," Freesen said quickly. Dykes nodded his agreement.

"Very well, begone, both of you!"

Ferguson reluctantly backed away and let the two men hurry out the doorway.

" 'Tis a sad thing to let those ruffians go with no punishment, my lord," Ferguson muttered, shaking his head.

"We could hardly let the world know that an Earl of Devbridge was a murderer, could we, Ferguson?" John asked reasonably.

To my chagrin, John's words began to lose meaning and substance. I reached out my hands, groping for something to support myself. Finding nothing, I slipped slowly to my knees and slumped forward. I felt strong arms lift me and set me on the cot.

"Do not become vaporish, my love, else I shall taunt you for the rest of our lives," John cajoled.

At his words, I tried to pull myself together, but everything was crumbling before me. He tried again, this time laughing. "Poor Ferguson. He has never been called a 'loathsome coward' before, particularly by such a diminutive little lady!"

This gave my mind focus and I remembered the man who had followed me to the lake. I looked toward the grinning Ferguson and inquired vaguely, "He was following me?"

"Protecting you," John corrected.

"Yes, milady, and a fine job of it I did until ye slipped out of your bedroom!" came Ferguson's hearty voice. He then shook his head. "I still can't figure out how your ladyship escaped."

"It was the narrow ledge outside my window," I answered mechanically. "But how did you find me?" I thought to ask.

"Oh, that" Ferguson answered cheerfully. "I was watching his lordship ride away with those men like the very devil was after 'em!"

John interjected. "I wasn't yet returned, so Ferguson followed them from a distance. When he saw you turn off to come to this cottage, he returned to the manor for me." He drew an audible breath. " I would never have left you, had I had any suspicion that my father would return so soon."

"I had been searching his rooms," I offered in a dazed voice.

"You what?" John asked incredulously.

I could not seem to manage an explanation, and despite my efforts, my eyes wandered unwillingly to where my father lay.

John quickly moved into my line of vision. He said brusquely, "It is time we left this place. Come, Andrea."

"But your arm . . ." I faltered, my eyes now straying to his blood-soaked shirt.

"It is nothing," he said as he gathered me into his arms.

NINE

"You are a bully and you have no right to give me orders!" I shouted.

"I beg to differ with you, my love. I have no intention to be married to a wraith, and if you don't drink this medicine, I shall force it down your throat," he threatened, standing over me.

Peter gave a shout of laughter. "Are you sure, Devbridge, that you wish to shackle yourself to such a spitfire?"

"It will be a sore trial, Jameson, of that I am certain." John grinned over his shoulder. "Now, madam," he said sternly, turning back to me.

"Oh, very well," I conceded, taking the glass from his hand. "But I think you are both abominable . . . autocratic . . ."

"Bullies," Peter supplied, grinning.

"On one condition," I qualified, eyeing the offending

potion with distaste. "A glass of port, else I shall accidentally tip this horrid valerian on the carpet!'

"She's got you there, John," Peter remarked appreciatively. "It is one of her more conventional habits," he added. He shook his head in mock despair.

"Peter, really!" I snapped crossly.

"Ah, Jameson, it this to be my future? Drinking port and smoking a cigar after dinner with a woman?" John looked the picture of a broken man.

"But, John," I protested, a twinkle in my eyes, "I have never been addicted to cigars. At least, not yet."

"I see now that I must beat her soundly, Jameson, if I am to have peace in my own house!"

"Either that or come back to Brussels with me," Peter offered cheerfully. He cocked an eyebrow at me. "I am acquainted with many . . . docile females," he added wickedly.

"Very tempting," John mused, gravely considering the matter. "But as a man of honor, I cannot in good conscience abandon her now. Despite her shrewish tongue, she would pine and wither away without me."

"The devil with both of you!" I cried peevishly, downing the medicine in one gulp and immediately falling into a paroxysm of coughing. My back was soundly thumped until the coughing subsided into a hiccup.

"My port," I demanded between hiccups.

"I am a beaten man, Jameson," John mourned as he poured the port and handed me the glass. I looked up at him and saw his eyes filled with such tenderness that I felt a lump rise in my throat.

Peter rose and stretched. "I really must be off. I promised to take Judith and Miss Gillbank out in the gig." He turned at the door. "Strive for a little conduct, sister," he admonished, and vanished before I could reply.

My chuckle at Peter's parting words turned to a nervous laugh and ended unromantically in a hiccup as John seated himself beside me and his arm touched my shoulders.

"John, your arm," I protested feebly.

"You know very well, goose, that my arm is perfectly healed," he retorted, pulling me against his shoulder.

"I shall spill my port," I said gruffly, all at once frightened and elated by his closeness.

"A problem easily solved," he replied smoothly. He removed the offending glass from my hand and set it on a table.

"Now . . ." He smiled tenderly at me, cupping my chin in his hand and lifting my face to his.

I stiffened ever so slightly as his lips touched mine, and he released me immediately. I felt a dull flush creep over my cheeks. Unable to meet his eyes, I looked resolutely at the top button of his waistcoat.

He ruffled my hair and said in an amused voice, "I shall have to stop wearing waistcoats if you find them more fascinating than their owner."

This brought a smile to my face, and I looked fleetingly up at him.

"That is much better," he nodded approvingly. After a slight pause he said gently, "You have naught to fear from me, my love, ever."

I looked away, confused and embarrassed by his forthrightness.

"Perhaps I should have waited for you to speak to me, but I did not. I have spoken with Peter, and he has told me much about your family . . . and your feelings."

He put his finger against my lips to silence my protest. I closed my eyes and leaned back against his shoulder.

"What is this?" he wondered aloud. "My Andrea silenced with but a touch of my finger?"

"You are a wretch, John," I cried indignantly, struggling impotently against his hold, only to realize that I was quite content that he did not release me. I felt sure that he must hear my heart, for it was beating wildly against my ribs. If he felt my response to him, he did not press me, but rather continued to hold me gently but firmly. Our silence was a comfortable one, broken only intermittently by the crackling logs spitting in the fireplace.

Perhaps the medicine loosened my tongue, but somehow at this moment it seemed important to me that I speak of Lawrence. In a voice of determined calm I began, "I have wanted to tell you, John, of the reasons for my marriage to your father."

"It is not necessary, Andrea, if you would rather not," he said earnestly. He pulled me away slightly so that he could see my face.

I gave my head a tiny shake. "I was afraid . . . afraid to give myself, as my mother had done. Peter guessed, and your father knew. Of course"—I faltered for a moment—"he agreed to a marriage of convenience for his own reasons." My eyes remained fastened on the brightly burning fire, and I felt somehow calmed by its warm glow.

"He would have raped me that last night, but something stopped him. Perhaps he saw my terror, perhaps he pitied me. I do not know . . ." My voice trailed off in a whisper, the memory vivid in my mind.

I felt him stiffen beside me, but after a moment he said in a gentle voice, "There is nothing more for you to tell me, Andrea. It is best forgotten, best that both of us forget."

But his effort to soothe me incensed me instead, for there remained a bitter memory that I could not forget. I had been honest with him, I reasoned to myself; could he not now be truthful with me? I turned and fixed him with a hard stare. He drew back and raised a black eyebrow questioningly.

"And you, John, can you so easily forget Lady Elizabeth?" I muttered stiffly.

The black eyebrow came down and he flashed a wide grin. "Truly a lovely woman, is she not?" he asked provocatively.

Bereft of speech, I pulled myself free, turned, and pounded his chest with my fists.

"Jealous, little cat?" he teased, as he locked my fists in his hands.

"You use me adominably," I complained, a sob catching in my throat.

"Use you?" he repeated, his voice incredulous.

"I do not find it at all amusing, John," I cried angrily. "I saw her go into your room!"

"What?" he demanded sharply.

I thrust my chin up and pursued defiantly, "I saw her go into your room the night of the ball."

He seemed to consider my words quite seriously for a moment before releasing my hands and leaning back against the sofa. His shoulders shook and his face was alight with laughter as he surveyed my angry face.

"My dearest love, who do you think received the young Duc de Chaillon's gallant attentions after you so callously cast him off?"

I pulled up short, my anger dissolving. "Why, it was Lady Elizabeth!" I cried happily, now remembering that they had left together the morning after the ball. I turned, and quite without thought threw my arms around his neck. He returned my embrace and pressed me tightly against his chest. I felt giddy with the new feelings that were racing through my body. His hands moved eagerly up my back, into my hair, pulling it free of the flimsy ribbon. I trembled as he pulled my arms from about his neck and cupped my chin in his hand. Willingly I let him bring his mouth to mine. I felt an uncontrollable quiver of desire as my lips parted under his gentle pressure and I felt his tongue mingle with mine. I could not help the soft moan of pleasure the escaped my lips.

Abruptly he clasped my arms in his hands and pulled me away from him. My startled eyes flew to his and soon filed fith tears of shame. I had thrown mystelf at him willingly, and yes, I had wanted him. I sat rigid and miserable, wondering what he must now think of me.

"Andrea, my love, you must forgive me. I must not, indeed, I will never take advantage of you again," he said softly. "At least," he amended, as I turned to him, now understanding, "not until we are married."

I gazed at him wide-eyed, not knowing how to respond to his words.

In an effort to break the intensity of the moment, he grinned at me wryly and asked in his lazy drawl of old "Are you sure, madam, that you wish to trust yourself to one whom you so profoundly distrusted but a short time ago?"

My lips parted in a quick smile. I meant to respond to him quite demurely, and was dismayed at the huskiness in my voice. "It seems such a long time ago. But it was your knife, my lord, was it not?" I countered.

"True," he admitted. He frowned a moment, and added in a thoughtful voice, "I, too, was at a loss to explain the knife, and the old woman, for that matter. I could see no reason for my father to have done that. Even later, I was surprised when Mrs. Eliott admitted that it was she."

"I tried to make her tell me earlier about the missing letters, but she was so terrified she would not speak."

He was smiling at me wonderingly. "You were certainly busy, were you not?"

"Yes," I retorted, "but it did not help one whit!" I furrowed my brow a moment, for there was something else I did not understand.

"John, she tried to warn me, in her own way, and I am certain that she always knew who I was. Did she know about Lady Caroline?"

"As a matter of fact, she did. In those days, she was Caroline's personal maid, and as I understand it, she was traveling with her on the Continent when Caroline met your father."

"No wonder she was terrified to speak. She feared your father all those years," I mused. "John, you will not send her away?"

He shook his head. "No, of course not. As you said, my love, she was trying to warn you without giving herself away."

I sighed wistfully and leaned back against John's arm. "Will anyone ever know about Lawrence's death? I mean, what really happened?"

John replied gravely, "Judith, certainly not. As for the magistrate, I have found him very understanding."

"Our neighbors?" I wondered aloud.

"Thomas and Amelia are busily informing everyone that he was killed . . . attempting to rescue you from kidnappers." He added thoughtfully. "Perhaps people will wonder, but they will have not one shred of proof to show otherwise."

"And my . . . father?" I whispered, trying not to remember him as last I had seen him.

"Andrea, don't think of it," he commanded sharply, shaking my shoulders gently. "Peter and I agreed that since his journey to England was a secret, there would be no inquiries from abroad." He added gently but with finality, "He was given an honourable burial in the Devbridge family cemetery."

Further conversation was interrupted by a sharp, insistent knocking on the door. I moved quickly away from John before calling out, "Enter."

Belinda bustled in, bearing a tea tray. At the sight of

my disheveled appearance, she sniffed audibly, a martial light in her eyes, and set the tray down heavily in front of me.

She straightened, arms akimbo, and glared meaningfully at John. Never one to mince matters, she declared, "After her ladyship has had her tea, my lord, she must rest before dinner!"

John nodded gravely, a twinkle in his eyes. "I am relieved that someone has your concern so much at heart." He rose and said blandly to Belinda, "Perhaps her ladyship can forgo tea. She has already evinced a strong interest to retire to bed."

I blushed scarlet and glared at him, speechless. He cocked an eyebrow, straightened his waistcoat, and strode from the room.

About the Author

Catherine Coulter was born and raised on a ranch in Texas and educated at the University of Texas and Boston College, a background which has left her equally fond of horseback riding, Baroque music, and European history. She has traveled widely and settled for a time in England and France, where she developed a special interest in Regency England and the Napoleonic era.

Today, Catherine Coulter is both a writer and a businesswoman, working in the Wall Street area of New York City. She lives in Manhattan with her husband, Dr. Anton Pogany, and is at present finishing work on her second novel.